"Nobody Even Has To Know You're Advising Me. It'll Be A Secret," Zach Offered.

Abby was having none of it. "So you can blackmail me with it later?" she challenged.

He gave an exaggerated eye-roll. "Don't be ridiculous."

"How is that ridiculous? You're blackmailing me now." Her voice came out more shrilly than she'd intended.

"There's only one thing I want from you, Abby."

"Don't call me Abby." That nickname was reserved for her family.

His gaze stayed on her, while he obviously regrouped. "How can we make this work?"

"You can go away and never come back."

He strode toward her, his normally laid-back style instantly bold, confident, purposeful. "I'm definitely not going away, Abigail. And from everything I've learned in the past week, you're the one person I need."

Dear Reader,

I've always been fascinated by the differing roles of family members and how those roles impact people's lives. It seems once expectations are set, brothers, sisters, mothers and fathers feel honor-bound to meet them.
In *An Intimate Bargain,* Abigail's family expects her unconditional support on the family cattle ranch. As an orphan, Zach doesn't understand her obligations. He only wants her to be happy, so he pushes her to pursue her own secret dreams.

I hope you enjoy the further adventures of the Jacobs and Terrell families in book three of Colorado Cattle Barons!

Enjoy!

Barbara Dunlop

BARBARA DUNLOP

AN INTIMATE BARGAIN

Harlequin®

Desire

Look for Barbara Dunlop's stunning conclusion
to Harlequin Desire's upcoming continuity
coming in December!

ISBN-13: 978-0-373-73171-8

AN INTIMATE BARGAIN

Copyright © 2012 by Barbara Dunlop

Recycling programs
for this product may
not exist in your area.

www.Harlequin.com

Printed in U.S.A.

Books by Barbara Dunlop

Harlequin Desire

An After-Hours Affair #2108
†*A Cowboy Comes Home* #2134
†*A Cowboy in Manhattan* #2140
†*An Intimate Bargain* #2158

Silhouette Desire

Thunderbolt over Texas #1704
Marriage Terms #1741
The Billionaire's Bidding #1793
The Billionaire Who Bought Christmas #1836
Beauty and the Billionaire #1853
Marriage, Manhattan Style #1897
Transformed Into the Frenchman's Mistress #1929
*Seduction and the CEO #1996
*In Bed with the Wrangler #2003
*His Convenient Virgin Bride #2009
The CEO's Accidental Bride #2062
Billionaire Baby Dilemma #2073

*Montana Millionaires: The Ryders
†Colorado Cattle Barons

Other titles by this author available in ebook format.

BARBARA DUNLOP

writes romantic stories while curled up in a log cabin in Canada's far north, where bears outnumber people and it snows six months of the year. Fortunately she has a brawny husband and two teenage children to haul firewood and clear the driveway while she sips cocoa and muses about her upcoming chapters. Barbara loves to hear from readers. You can contact her through her website, www.barbaradunlop.com.

For my husband

One

The last time Zach Rainer felt this level of anxiety, he was walking out of a Texas group home on his eighteenth birthday. Twelve years later, there was more than just his future at stake.

He'd been navigating the Interstate since dawn in his three-year-old Jaguar convertible with nothing but a stale truck stop sandwich and six cardboard cups of coffee to keep him going. His business partner, Alex Cable, had insisted the road trip from Texas to Colorado would clear his head. Zach should have known better. Thinking didn't solve problems, action did.

Now he checked himself into the Caspian Hotel in downtown Lyndon, Colorado, and accepted his key to an eighth-floor room. While he pocketed his credit card, his attention was drawn to the mezzanine level that overlooked the atrium lobby. Sharply dressed men and glittering ladies circulated at the top of a grand, curving staircase, while chamber music sounded around them.

He put the room key in his pocket and left his bags with the porter. Tugging the sleeves of his travel-worn blazer, he took the friendly clerk's advice and started for a sports-bar down the hall. The woman had assured him it would be a lot less crowded there. Though, given his wrinkled shirt and day's growth of beard, he was guessing she thought he'd fit in better with the sports bar crowd. Not that he cared about making any kind of impression. He was too tired and too hungry to worry about anything more than a hot meal and a long night's sleep.

Tomorrow morning, he'd drive up into the hills behind Lyndon to the Craig Mountain Brewery and take stock of the place. Craig Mountain was the weak link in DFB Incorporated, the microbrewery conglomerate that he and Alex had grown over the past twelve years. At the same time, Craig Mountain had suddenly become the potential salvation of the entire corporation and the hundreds of jobs that went with it.

At the end of the hall, he entered the dimly lit bar through a lighted archway. He blinked to adjust his eyes, then he zeroed in on an empty table across from the wide-screen television. A basketball game was playing, the announcer's words scrolling in closed caption across the bottom of the screen, while an eighties rock tune came through speakers high in the corners of the room.

It was Lakers versus Celtics. Neither were teams he followed, but watching the action would help his mind rest up for tomorrow. Production at Craig Mountain was currently ten thousand barrels per year. In order to save DFB, he needed to triple that in the next six months.

As he rounded the polished bar, his attention was snagged by a startlingly beautiful, auburn-haired woman. Perched on a leather chair, she was alone at a table and looked seriously out of place in the casual atmosphere. She wore a low-cut, black cocktail dress with spaghetti straps over her smooth shoulders. It clung to her body in a drop waist, then layered out into a full skirt, ending at midthigh.

Her graceful, lavender-tipped fingers were wrapped around the martini glass in front of her. She was obviously deep in thought, her attention fixed on a spot on the far wall. The flickering light from the television highlighted her compelling hazel eyes. They were streaked with gold, mesmerizing and undeniably sexy. Her hair was pulled back in a wavy updo, a few loose strands artfully arranged at her temples, brushing against dangling crystal earrings.

Zach's feet came to an automatic halt, and he couldn't seem to stop himself from gaping at her beauty. She glanced up and caught him, drawing back in surprise. He knew what she must be thinking, and immediately opened his mouth to apologize.

But to his surprise, she smiled and nodded a greeting.

Zach might be exhausted and starving, but he still had a pulse. He wasn't about to walk away from a reception like that.

"Hello," he offered, seizing the opportunity to ease closer to her table.

"Getting away from the crowd?" she asked, her deep red lips curving into a friendly, open smile.

He nodded. "They told me it would be quieter back here."

"Well, a different kind of noise anyway," she acknowledged with a wry glance at the speakers.

Zach had to grin at that. "Not my favorite, either."

"At least the crowd is thinner."

"Agreed," he replied.

"My face was about to crack from all that smiling."

"You're smiling now," he pointed out, taking the final couple of steps that brought him to the chair opposite her. He rested his hand on its back.

"I guess I am." She tipped her head quizzically, and her beautiful, golden eyes narrowed. "I don't remember meeting you at the reception."

Zach knew he was about to be outed as a stranger. He also knew he had about two seconds to figure out a way to prolong the conversation. He boldly pulled out the chair and slid into it.

"That's because you didn't meet me." He took a stab in the dark. "Are you a friend of the bride?"

"What bride?"

Damn. Okay, that was a huge miss. And he couldn't think of anywhere else to go but the truth. "I confess. I wasn't at the reception."

"You mean you're not here to celebrate Mayor Seth Jacobs' election victory?"

"I am not," he admitted, holding her gaze.

She squinted with suspicion. "You have anything against Mayor Jacobs?"

"I do not. I've never met the man."

Her face relaxed at that. Her shoulders drooped a little, and she leaned back into the big, brown leather chair.

Zach knew he was about to get his marching orders. Too bad. He'd have loved to sit here and get to know this woman, even if it did mean forgoing the burger and fries he'd promised his empty stomach.

"So you don't know who I am?" she asked.

"I'd like to," Zach immediately put in.

She chuckled. "While I'd prefer it if you had no earthly idea."

He didn't miss a beat. His tone went low and intimate as he propped his elbows on the lacquered tabletop and leaned toward her. "I can live with that, too."

She rested her own elbows on the table, leaning forward, a playful glint now lurking in her expression. "I wasn't offering to date you."

"I didn't think you were." He quickly backed off. Okay, he'd hoped she was. But a guy could hope without penalty.

"Are you lying?" she asked him.

"I am not."

She contemplated him a moment longer. "I take it you're not from Lyndon."

"No, ma'am."

"Passing through?"

"Essentially." He hoped he wouldn't have to stay long. He hoped tripling production at Craig Mountain proved to be a straightforward proposition, that he could leave the brewery manager with instructions for expansion then get himself back to his corporate headquarters in Houston. He'd left Alex to hold down the fort during a very critical time.

Her sexy fingertips drummed lightly against the table. "So, we could do this?"

"Do what?" He found himself hoping all over again, but he sure wasn't going to presume a second time.

"Have a casual conversation about nothing that matters. You don't know me. I don't know you."

"Absolutely," he agreed without hesitation. He could talk with her, or do absolutely anything else that she wanted.

Someone entered the bar through the archway, drawing her attention. She tracked the progress of a fiftysomething man as he headed for the bar. After a few seconds, she seemed to relax. She turned back to Zach.

"Waiting for someone?" he couldn't help asking.

She emphatically shook her head.

His second guess would be that she was avoiding someone. He took a chance on his instincts. "You want to get out of here?"

She seemed to contemplate his words for a long, slow moment. "Yes," she finally answered. "I believe I do."

He gestured with a tilt of his head. "I saw an exit door at the far end of that hall. We can probably make a clean getaway."

"What makes you think I need a getaway?"

He leaned across the table again, dramatically lowering his voice. "You're acting like someone who needs to lie low for a while."

She matched his posture once more. "You make me sound like a felon."

"Are you a felon?"

She fought a grin. "Would it matter?"

"No," he answered honestly. With her looks and sense of humor, it truly would not.

She chuckled low, drew back and rose from her chair, retrieving a small, black clutch. "Then let's do it."

He stood with her. She moved past him, and the exotic scent of jasmine teased his senses.

He inhaled appreciatively then affected a Chicago-gangster drawl. "Act natural, Doll-Face, and stick close to me."

She matched his tone. "Right beside you...Lucky."

He couldn't help grinning to himself as they crossed the bar. He lowered his voice. "You want I should score us a getaway car?"

"We're only half a block from Main Street," she stage-whispered in return. "Plenty of hideouts there."

They ducked into the hallway then hurried for the back exit. Zach pushed the heavy, steel door open, and they crossed the threshold into the late-summer night. The door clanged shut behind them.

"A clean break," she breathed, pressing her back dramatically against the brick wall.

"Stick with me, Doll-Face," he rumbled in return, making a show of checking both directions on the quiet street. "I don't see any gumshoes hanging around."

"Good to know. But I'm more worried about constituents."

"Constituents?" He played dumb. "You mean the feds?"

She shifted away from the wall and started down the short block toward Main Street, her high heels echoing on the pavement. "I mean the good people of Lyndon. I don't want anyone to recognize me."

"So I'm hiding you from the entire town?" he asked with mock incredulity.

"Only from the people I know."

"How many people do know you?"

"Several thousand."

He fought what seemed like a natural urge to fold her hand into his. "You don't make things easy on a guy," he grumbled instead.

"You seem pretty good at this," she responded, glancing up. "You sure you're not a real criminal?"

"I'm a businessman." As soon as the words were out of his mouth, he realized they made him sound like a character from *The Godfather*. "A legitimate one," he added. But that wasn't much better. "I don't have so much as a parking ticket," he finished, hoping he hadn't scared her off.

"What kind of—" But then she determinedly shook her head. "Nope. I don't want to know what you do."

The wind had picked up, lifting the loose strands of her hair. He resisted an urge to reach out and smooth them back. "Can we at least trade first names?"

She hesitated, a look of consternation crossing her face. Then, just as quickly, she grinned. "Call me Doll-Face."

He paused as they reached the curb, half turning to offer a handshake. "Call me Lucky."

She glanced at his hand briefly, then reached out to wrap her delicate fingers over his rough skin. "Hello, Lucky." Her sweet voice seemed to touch a place deep inside him and settled there.

He let their handshake lengthen, having absolutely no desire to let her go.

Abigail Jacobs didn't usually flirt. She rarely had the inclination and, lately, she certainly hadn't had the time. But tonight was different. Her life was about to take a dramatic U-turn, and she didn't want to face the change just yet. Joking with Lucky was keeping the future at bay.

After tonight, she'd no longer be Abigail Jacobs, sister and campaign manager to mayoral candidate Seth Jacobs. She wouldn't be running the campaign office, picking up the phone to call business owners and reporters. She wouldn't polish speeches, organize events, manage budgets and head off crises. Tomorrow morning she'd pack away her dressy clothes, turn in her office keys, give up the leased Audi and leave Lyndon City in a dusty, ranch pickup truck.

Growing up, she'd loved her ranch life, the freedom, the fresh air and open spaces. But somewhere along the way, the city had sunk its hooks in her, making her wish for things she couldn't have. With her sister Mandy recently engaged to their former neighbor Caleb Terrell, and similarly, her other sister Katrina engaged to Caleb's brother, Reed, her father and mother in Houston working on his stroke recovery and her brother Seth now the mayor of Lyndon, she couldn't abandon her other brother, Travis, to manage the ranch alone.

Like it or not, the ball was ending, and tomorrow morning Cinderella was going back to the dust and manure of the real world.

"Hungry?" asked Lucky beside her, his coffee-colored eyes warm in the glow of the streetlights.

"Sure." It had been quite a while since Abigail had eaten. In a rush this morning, she'd skipped breakfast, and she'd been too nervous to eat all day. When the polls finally closed at dinnertime, the entire team had waited with bated breath for the vote count.

Of course, there'd been food at tonight's victory party, but there she'd been too busy fielding congratulations and questions about her future plans to eat anything. She'd told everyone she was looking forward to going home to the family ranch. After about the hundredth lie, she'd made her escape to the hotel sports bar.

"Steak?" Lucky asked with a nod toward the glowing red sign for Calbert's.

She shook her head. "Too many people I'll know in there."

"Thai?" he suggested, zeroing in on a smaller, lower-key restaurant a few doors down.

"How about a burger from the drive-through?"

Bert's Burgers, half a block down in the other direction, catered mostly to a teenage crowd. Much as they'd tried to get out the youth vote, Abigail doubted anyone under the age of twenty-one would recognize her.

"We don't have a car," Lucky pointed out.

"We can walk to the drive-through and take the burgers down to the lake."

He arched a skeptical brow. "You sure?"

She nodded.

There were some picnic tables on the lawn by the beach. The election party fireworks finale was planned for later on the waterfront. But it would take place on the wharf at the opposite end of the bay. This time of night, their only company in the picnic area would be the mallard ducks that slept in the marsh.

"Not much of a date," he noted as they took advantage of a break in traffic to cross in the middle of the block.

She couldn't help smiling at that. "This is a date?"

"Not in my book."

"So why are you worrying about the aesthetics?"

They stepped up on the sidewalk on the other side of the street.

"Because you're wearing a two-thousand-dollar dress, and I'm buying you a burger and fries."

"Who says you're buying?"

"I'm from Texas."

She smacked her hands dramatically over her ears, signaling her unwillingness to learn where he was from. "La, la, la, la—"

He playfully pulled one of them away. "You can already tell that by my accent."

"Just because you grew up in Texas doesn't mean you live there now."

"I do."

"Quit breaking the rules," she warned him.

"There are rules?"

"Yes, there are rules. We agreed."

"Well, the rule in Texas is that a gentleman always buys a lady's dinner."

"This is Colorado."

They came to a halt beside the drive-through window, and he peered up at the lighted menu board. "And this isn't exactly dinner."

A teenage girl in a navy-blue-and-white uniform, her hair pulled back in a ponytail revealing purple beaded earrings, slid the window open. "What'll you have?"

"A mountain burger," Abigail decided. "No onions, extra tomato and a chocolate shake."

"Same for me," said Lucky, extracting his wallet. "But I'll take some fries with that."

Abigail decided not to press the issue of payment. What point would she be making? That she was an independent woman? That this wasn't a date? Date or not, she doubted a five-dollar dinner would make any man feel entitled to so much as a good-night kiss.

Not that she'd necessarily mind kissing Lucky. She found herself stealing a glance at his profile while he handed the girl a twenty. He was an incredibly attractive man. As tall as her brothers, easily over six feet. He had gorgeous brown eyes, thick, dark hair, full lips, a straight nose, with a square chin that was slightly beard shadowed. He wasn't cowboy. She'd call it urbane. With an edge. She liked that.

"Cherry turnover?" he asked, turning to catch her staring.

She quickly blinked away her curiosity. "No, thanks."

"We're good," he said to the girl.

The cashier rang their purchase through the register, handing him the change, while another employee appeared with a white paper bag of food and a cardboard tray holding two milk shakes and paper-covered straws.

Lucky took the bag in one hand, the milk shakes in the other. "Lead on."

"You want some help?"

"I've got it."

"Texans don't let women carry things?"

"No, ma'am."

Abigail couldn't help wondering what he'd think of her hauling hay bales and lumber, and hefting saddles back at the ranch. Then she compressed her lips, determinedly banishing the image. That would be her life tomorrow. For tonight, she was going to be a girlie girl, with makeup, jewelry, horribly impractical shoes and a Texas man who insisted on buying her dinner.

"This way," she told him with determined cheer.

They headed for the lighted, bark-mulch path that led from the side of the parking lot down to the beach and picnic area. They made their way beneath the glow of overhead lights and the rustle of aspens and sugar maple trees. Her narrow, three-inch heels sank into the loose bark mulch of the pathway. After stumbling a few times, she moved to one side, stopped and slipped off the shoes to stand barefoot on the lush lawn.

Lucky halted to check on her. "You okay there?"

"I'm fine." She picked up the sandals, dangling them from the straps, the grass cool and soft against her soles.

"Is it safe to walk barefoot?"

"The park's well maintained."

He frowned in obvious concern. "I could give you a lift."

"Is that how they do it in Texas? Haul their women around over their shoulders?"

"When necessary."

"It's not necessary. I've been running barefoot through this park since I was two years old."

"You sure?"

"I'm sure." She began walking, passing him. "But thank you," she added belatedly, turning to pace backward so she could watch him.

He had a long, easy stride. His shirt collar was open. She could see the fabric was wrinkled, but his blazer was well cut, delineating broad, and what she guessed were well-muscled, shoulders. She wondered if he also had a six-pack.

"You grew up in Lyndon?" he asked.

"I did."

Technically her family's ranch was two hours west of Lyndon. But she wasn't going to fret over the details. Tonight she was a city girl through and through.

"Brothers and sisters?" he asked.

"Both. You?" She didn't think the question would take them too far down the road to revealing their identities. Mainly, she didn't want him to know she was the mayor's sister, and she didn't want him to know she was really a ranch hand.

He shook his head. "Nope."

"You were an only child?"

"That's right. Watch where you're going."

She turned her head to discover they were only a few feet from the first picnic table. The grass was about to give way to sand.

"Perfect," she pronounced, dropping her sandals to the ground and stepping up on the wooden bench seat, intending to perch on the tabletop facing the lake.

"Hold up there." Lucky swiftly set down the burgers. Stripping off his blazer, he laid it down like a blanket for her to sit on. The simple gesture made her chest tighten.

"Gotta love Texans," she joked, taking in the breadth of his chest beneath the thin, white cotton shirt. The fabric was tight over his biceps, and she was more willing than ever to lay a bet on him having six-pack abs.

"Can't have you ruining your dress," he said.

"So we're going to ruin your jacket instead?" But she sat down on the warm satin lining.

He shrugged, plunking down beside her, placing the burgers and shakes between them.

A couple of fat mallards splashed and waddled their way out of the water, crossing the pebbles and sand to investigate their presence, obviously on the lookout for bread crumbs.

Lucky handed her a foil-wrapped burger. "The jacket will clean."

"So would the dress."

He simply shrugged again.

The wrapper crackled as she peeled it halfway down the thick burger. Then Lucky was handing her a shake with a plastic straw already sticking through the lid.

She transferred the burger to the opposite hand as she accepted the drink, taking a sip of the icy, smooth treat.

"Yum," she acknowledged, then took a bite of the burger. It was juicy and flavorful, with a fresh bun and crisp condiments. Her stomach rumbled quietly in anticipation.

"I'm starving," she muttered around the bite.

"Me, too," he agreed with a nod, digging in to his own burger. "Long day on the road."

"Long day in the office for me."

Then they both ate in silence, while a few more ducks made their way over from a small, reed-filled marsh. Abigail tossed them some bits of bun, and they quacked with excitement, wings flapping, orange beaks pecking the ground.

Satiated, she took a long drink of the milk shake and threw the remains of her bun to the birds.

"Better?" asked Lucky, crumpling his wrapper and tossing it into the empty bag. She tucked hers away, as well, and he set the trash behind them.

"Much better," she acknowledged.

His gaze settled on the black horizon, where the moon was

coming up over the mountains, fading the stars that were scattered across the sky. "So, are you going to tell me?"

"Tell you what?"

"What's going on here?"

She waggled her cardboard cup at him, pretending to misunderstand his question. "I'm finishing my milk shake."

"That's not what I meant."

"Then what did you mean?"

"You must have guys hitting on you all the time."

Abigail coughed out a laugh. "Not really."

She'd spent most of her life in dusty blue jeans, hair in a sensible ponytail, face free of makeup while she worked up a sweat on the land. Things had been slightly different during the campaign. But most of the attention had been on her brother Seth, and most of the people she spoke to in Lyndon remembered her as a little freckle-faced, red-haired girl with pigtails and skinned knees.

Lucky gazed down at her. "First of all, I don't believe you. Second, I'm betting you don't usually accept dinner invitations from strange men."

She took a long, noisy slurp, draining the milk shake. "I do when it's a mountain burger."

He gently removed the cup from her hand, setting it on the table behind them. "Spill, Doll-Face. Who are you hiding from?"

"That's a stupid name." But she couldn't seem to tear her gaze from his.

"Then tell me your real name."

"No." She was enjoying this anonymity. For a brief space of time, she wasn't Seth's campaign manager, or Travis's stalwart sister and ranch hand. She was her own woman, nothing more, nothing less.

"Then Doll-Face is all I've got." Lucky's smooth baritone rolled over her like warm honey.

It really was a silly name, but when he said it, it sounded sweet. He reached up and brushed a strand of hair back from her forehead, and her skin tingled behind the touch.

"Don't do that." She closed her eyes, hiding her emotion as the incredible sensation slowly ebbed.

"Sorry."

She shook her head, regretting the sharpness of her outburst. "Don't worry about it."

"You had to know I was attracted to you."

Had to? No. Suspected? Sure. She wasn't stupid.

After a long moment, he spoke again. "So why'd you come with me?"

She opened her eyes, and it was her turn to drink in the blackened horizon and the sharpening moon. She hesitated to tell him anything remotely close to the truth, but reality had been burning in her brain all evening long, and it seemed desperate to get out. "Because I'm putting off tomorrow," she told him on a sigh. "It's going to be a very bad day."

She expected him to press for details, was already weighing exactly how much she'd say.

But he didn't ask. Instead, he shifted, and the wooden table creaked beneath his weight. "I hear you." He paused. "There's a better-than-even chance that my tomorrow's going to suck, too."

Despite herself, he had her curious. She turned to take in his profile. "Yeah?"

He set aside his own cardboard cup. "Yeah."

"Family?" she probed, promising herself, whatever it was, she'd keep the conversation to generalities.

He shook his head.

"Girlfriend?" she dared, swallowing a sudden lump.

He turned to paste her with a scowl. "While I'm hitting on you? Thanks tons, Doll-Face."

She tried not to feel quite so relieved. "Gambling, drinking, illness?"

"Business," he answered, his tone smoothing out. "There's a problem with my mysterious, yet perfectly legitimate, business interests. But I take it your problem is family?"

"What makes you say that?"

"It was your first guess for me. That makes it top of your mind."

She took in his expression, seeing warmth and compassion and, yes, a little bit of lust. But she was okay with that. It had taken her two hours to dress up for the reception tonight. It was nice to know somebody appreciated her efforts.

Her first instinct was to evade his question. But for some reason, she wanted to be honest with him. "My family needs me to do one thing," she told him. "But I want to do something else entirely."

He canted his head, and he suddenly seemed closer, his chest looked broader, his voice going lower. "Age-old dilemma," he rumbled.

She picked up his woodsy musk scent, getting lost in his warm, brown eyes, and momentarily lost brain function. She braced her hand on the tabletop, gripping with her fingertips. "I guess."

"So what are you going to do?"

She blinked. It wasn't like there was a choice. "Support my family."

The pad of his thumb passed over her knuckles, sending a kick of reaction up her spine. He gave a small smile. "I'd have guessed that about you, Doll-Face. You seem like the loyal type."

"What about you?" she managed to say around a drying throat and laboring breaths. Every single thing about this man oozed sex appeal. "What would you do?"

His hand covered hers completely, warm, broad and strong. "I'd make my own choice. I'd do whatever I wanted."

She was surprised, but also intrigued. "Even if it hurt your family?"

"My family doesn't need me."

"Mine needs me."

"Are you sure about that?"

"Positive."

He lifted an index finger to touch the bottom of her chin.

This time, she didn't wave him off. She drank in the sensation of his touch, anticipating the kiss that was sure to come.

What would it hurt?

What could it hurt?

Tomorrow she'd be back in her blue jeans, and men like Lucky wouldn't give her the time of day. Surely she deserved one single kiss.

Two

Zach figured there was a pretty good chance he was about to get his face slapped. He also figured it was going to be worth it.

He leaned in, anticipating her taste, the softness of her full lips. But a boat horn suddenly blasted from the lake, and Doll-Face abruptly turned away. Then another horn sounded, and another.

Disappointment clenched Zach's gut, even as light and color flashed in the periphery of his vision. He looked toward the lake in time to see starbursts of color cascading in the skies above.

A cheer went up from the crowd that had gathered far down the shore and out onto the wharf. A few people had also arrived in the park, taking up spots on nearby picnic tables. Zach hadn't even noticed them.

Doll-Face settled back to watch the show, bracing her hands and locking her elbows, bringing her dress taut against her breasts, highlighting an intriguing dip of cleavage.

Her skin was honey-toned with a tan. Her neck was long and graceful, her face classically beautiful, with big, golden eyes, dark lashes and a wide, sexy smile.

"Wow," she whispered. "That's spectacular."

"It sure is," he agreed, gaze fully on her, still desperate to lean down and kiss her mouth. Her auburn hair was slightly mussed. Wisps had worked their way free from the updo, along her neck and forehead. He had a sudden vision of her lying back on a white pillowcase, naked, thoroughly kissed, a sheen of sweat glistening on her brow.

He gave himself a shake.

"Oooh," she sang, smiling. Then she glanced up at him. "You're missing it."

He wasn't missing a thing. But he turned to look at the fireworks anyway. "Part of the election celebration?"

"It is," she said. "I should be standing out there on the dock with a glass of champagne in my hand, toasting my—"

He waited, but she didn't add anything to the end of the sentence. "You want to go drink some champagne?" he felt compelled to ask. The last thing he wanted to do was join the crowd down the beach.

"No. I was just wondering if anyone noticed I was missing."

"Did you have a date at the party?" That could easily have been the end of her sentence. Toasting with her boyfriend? Was that what she'd meant to say?

He glanced reflexively at her left hand. No ring. At least she hadn't been talking about toasting with her fiancé.

"No date," she assured him.

He scanned his way from her knees to her breasts, along her neck, returning to her face. Bursts of light danced off her skin, reflecting in her gorgeous eyes. His voice went husky. "Do you have a boyfriend?"

She met his gaze for a long moment, while he tensed, waiting. Then she shook her head. "Not since Russell Livingston, senior year."

"How old are you?"

"How old do I look?"

"Young enough that I should ask."

She grinned. "I'm twenty-six."

He did the math. "So you haven't had a boyfriend in four years?" He found that absolutely impossible to believe. What on earth was wrong with the men of Colorado?

"Not a steady one." She gave a little lift of her chin. "How about you?"

"I've never had a boyfriend."

She threw an elbow to his rib cage. "You know what I mean, Lucky."

He steadied her arm with his hand as she rocked back. "Nobody serious."

She resettled her bare feet on the picnic-table bench. "Since when?"

He reluctantly removed his hand from her arm, shrugging as he took in the glinting copper polish on her toenails. Sexy. How had he missed that up to now? "Since forever."

"You've never been in love?"

"I've never been in love," he confirmed. He'd never had the time. Not that he'd be likely to recognize it if it happened. He'd had no role models, no examples of romantic love in his formative years. He supposed he loved Alex like a brother. But that was a completely different thing.

"Me neither," said Doll-Face. She contemplated the fireworks display for a minute. "But both of my sisters are in love."

"You have two sisters?"

"And two brothers."

"Are your parents still together?"

Her expression faltered for a second, but then she nodded, voice a little quieter. "Yes, they are. And they're still very much in love."

"Sounds like a perfect family." Reflexive resentment flickered inside Zach. But he quickly tamped it down. He wouldn't wish his tough childhood on anyone, least of all this delightful, beautiful creature in front of him.

She laughed. "We're a long, long way from perfect. But there's a wedding coming up. A double wedding."

"Both sisters?" he guessed.

"I'll be the maid of honor." Then she sniffed and wrinkled her nose. "And me, the oldest."

"Oh, that's not good." Zach shook his head in mock concern. "Tragic, really. Pitiful."

"Isn't it?"

"An old maid at twenty-six." He clicked his cheek. "What will the neighbors say?"

Her laughter tinkled. "They'll probably introduce me to every eligible bachelor they can lay their hands on."

Zach knew she was probably right. And he didn't like that image. He had a sudden urge to curl an arm around her, pull her close, tell her to stay away from all those no-good bachelors.

"Funny," she continued, her gaze back on the fireworks. "Marriage has never been a goal of mine."

"Mine, neither," Zach agreed, ridiculously relieved. It was silly, stupid even. He didn't know the woman's name, yet he didn't want to think about her with other men.

"What *is* your goal?" he prompted. The gasps of the crowd and the pops of the rockets once again penetrated his conscious, reminding him of where they were.

She shrugged her slim, bare shoulders. "A career, maybe."

"What kind of career?" This line of conversation definitely beat talking about her future boyfriends.

"Lately I've been thinking about event management, or maybe business."

"What's your degree in?"

"History. Don't you dare laugh."

Did she mean at the impracticality of studying history? "I'm not laughing. I don't even have a college degree."

She waited for him to continue. There was no judgment in her expression.

"Where I come from," he found himself explaining, "high school graduation is about as far as kids go."

"Did you graduate high school?"

"I did." He paused. "But would you care if I hadn't?" He was honestly curious.

"I don't think it's your education that matters. It's what you do with it."

He couldn't agree more.

With the exception of their accountant, DFB Incorporated didn't have a single employee with a college degree. Mostly because they were all foster kids. They'd grown up in group homes, like him, or in a series of short-term, single-family placements. They'd learned to avoid emotional attachment to their caregivers and had spent their childhoods in survival mode. None of them had family ties. None would have had a single penny of support, even if they had wanted to go to college.

"If you want to use your history degree to go into business," he told her, "I'm all for it."

She smiled, and his chest tightened. "Thank you."

He drew a couple of hard breaths. He'd never wanted to kiss a woman quite this badly. But people could see them, and she was trying to keep a low profile. "What kind of business?" he forced himself to ask again.

"I haven't the slightest idea."

"Well, if you start your own, expand slowly. Make sure you don't overleverage."

"Is that what you did?" There was an astute intelligence in those golden eyes. It was as if she'd suddenly shifted modes, staring frankly, seeking information.

Okay, that really shouldn't strike him as sexy.

"We grew fast," he told her, shifting his attention to the lake in order to keep from grabbing her right here in front of everyone. "When you hit a certain size, all of a sudden there are a whole lot of moving parts. We ended up with a weak link. And I'm here to fix it." It seemed silly to stay so oblique. "You want me to tell you what the—"

"No!" It was her hand on his arm more than her words that shut him up.

He glanced down at her slim fingers, the lavender polish, felt the heat through the thin cotton of his shirt, and thought about all the other places he'd like her to touch him.

"It's better this way," she assured him.

It would be better with her in his arms.

The sky suddenly lit up with the fireworks finale. The crowd oohed then aahed then cheered madly as the sky went dark.

"Whatever you want," Zach told her, meaning it in all possible ways.

* * *

Abigail knew the evening had to come to an end. It was after three in the morning. They'd been talking for hours, and she was nearly asleep on her feet as they approached the front entrance of the Caspian Hotel.

Except for the doorman, the place was deserted. He tipped his hat, gave them a welcoming smile and opened the glass-fronted, brass-trimmed door so they could enter.

Lucky slowed his steps and motioned with an outstretched arm for Abigail to go in first. Her heels clicked on the marble floor, echoing through the empty lobby. A front-desk clerk glanced up from her computer screen. Seeing they had no luggage, so obviously weren't checking in, she nodded a greeting and went back to typing on the keyboard.

They crossed the vast lobby toward the bank of elevators, while Abigail struggled for something clever or memorable to say. But everything she came up with sounded either trite or ridiculous.

Lucky pressed the call button, and an elevator door immediately slid open. She wanted to tell him she'd had a great time. No, not a great time, an amazing time. A time that she wished she could repeat again someday. But she knew that was impossible. He was leaving town. And she was going back to her real life. And she didn't even know his name.

He pressed eight, then lifted his brows in her direction.

"Same," she confirmed, her voice raspy over her dry throat.

Their gazes locked, and the air in the elevator seemed to thicken with anticipation.

The door slid shut.

"Imagine that," Lucky observed.

Abigail's skin tingled. She felt heat rush up from her toes to her scalp. She'd never, ever, not even once, had a one-night stand. But she was tempted tonight.

The elevator pinged to a stop.

The door slid open.

She exited first, turning left down the hallway, wondering

what she could say, if she could say it, if she could possibly, actually bring herself to do it.

He fell into step, the heat from his body seeming to swirl out to touch her.

"Eight-nineteen," he told her, extracting his key card, slowing to a stop.

"Eight-twenty," she responded, stopping beside him.

He glanced down.

She looked up.

Her heart pounded hard against the inside of her chest. A roaring sound filled her ears. And her lungs labored as she moistened her dry lips.

He cocked his head ever so slightly toward his hotel-room door. "I'm thinking there'll be a bottle of wine in my minibar."

Abigail tried to make her head shake no, but somehow the message got scrambled. "Red or white?" she rasped instead.

"Either. Both. Whatever you want."

She knew she should say good-night and leave. This was her last chance. If she walked into that hotel room, she would throw herself into Lucky's arms, damn the consequences.

She couldn't tell him no. But she couldn't bring herself to say yes either.

He slipped the key into the lock, and the indicator light turned green. He pushed down on the handle, released the latch and yawned the door wide open.

Abigail took one step then another into his room, her shoes whispering against the thick carpet. The door whooshed shut behind them, clicking with finality.

From behind, Lucky gently touched her shoulder. He turned her, backed her slowly against the closed door, one hand tunneling into her hair, the other coming around her waist, pressing their bodies together while his lips came down on hers. They were firm, hot, moist and tender.

She gave in to the sensation, immediately kissing him back, grasping his arms, steadying herself against the steel of his biceps. She opened wide, welcoming his tongue, marveling at his sweet taste, his masculine scent and the feel of his thighs hard against her own.

He broke the kiss, speaking huskily against her lips. "I've been dying to do that all night long."

"Are we crazy?" she felt compelled to ask, lips hot and swollen, desire permeating every cell of her body.

He captured her gaze once more. "I don't particularly care."

She couldn't help smiling at that. "Am I going to sound preposterous if I say I've never done anything like this before?"

"You haven't done anything yet."

"I'm about to."

"Yeah?"

"Yeah."

"Glad to hear it." He kissed her again, longer and deeper, his fingertips finding their way up her spine.

She wrapped her arms around his neck, tipping back, abandoning herself to the passion building inside her body. She was an adult woman. She wasn't reckless, and she wasn't foolish. She'd thought this through, and she wanted to be with Lucky tonight.

"You're gorgeous," he whispered, smoothing his hand along her shoulder. He pushed her shoulder strap out of the way. Then he tenderly kissed her shoulder and eased the other strap down. "Amazing," he mumbled, kissing his way along her neck. The back of his knuckles brushed the tip of her breast, and she sucked in a breath in response. "I am the luckiest guy on the planet."

"Is that why they call you Lucky?"

He stilled, lips brushing against the tender hollow of her neck. "You're making a joke?"

"I am," she offered without a trace of apology.

He kissed her again, more firmly this time, drawing her tongue into his scorching mouth. "Well, I'm not going to keep calling you Doll-Face."

"Oh, yes, you are."

"What's your real name?"

"Uh-uh." She shook her head.

"You sure about that?"

"I'm sure."

His hands slid their way down to her wrists, and he backed her tighter against the door. "Okay. Then that's pretty hot."

She tipped her chin. "You're pretty hot."

"I'm about to get hotter." His eyes turned to molten chocolate, and a split second later he was kissing her mouth, harder, deeper. One hand slipped up her back, finding her zipper, pulling it down. The tight bodice gave way.

In return, she reached for his shirt buttons, plunking the disks through the open holes, revealing his chest, running her fingers over his bare skin.

He gave a tug on her dress, and it slid to the floor, freeing her bare breasts and pooling in a heap around her feet.

He drew back, his breath whistling out. "Where have you been hiding all my life?"

"Colorado." She pulled his shirttails out of his pants, and stripped the shirt off his shoulders.

He was absolutely magnificent, and they both stilled, staring at each other in silence.

He lifted his broad hand, cupping her face with his palm, leaning in ever so slowly. Her eyes fluttered closed. She inhaled deeper. Her lips parted, and she eased toward him, twining her arms around his neck, feeling his heated skin press tight against her breasts, as his lips came down in a tender kiss that drew itself out for long minutes.

His free hand slipped over the curve of her hip. There, his fingers paused, slipping beneath the strand of her panties. His other hand slid up to cup her breast. Her nipples instantly beaded, and his palm closed around her. His kisses grew more insistent, longer, until they were both gasping for breath.

He kissed her neck, dipping to a breast, drawing the taut nipple into his mouth. Her hands fisted hard, and she moaned at a sensation she'd never experienced. What was he doing? How was he doing it?

Cool air replaced the heat of his mouth, and she loved the

contrast. He switched to the other breast, causing cascades of desire to roll through her.

She needed to do something.

She was just standing here.

She ran her palms up his chest, feeling the burn of his skin, testing the muscles she knew would be steel hard. Then she worked her way down, over the six-pack of his abs, to the waistband of his pants, popping the button and lowering his zipper.

He grabbed her wrist. "I want this to go slow."

"Sure," she agreed, even though her mind screamed for speed. She brushed her knuckles against him.

"You want it slow?" he growled.

"No."

He stilled for a second. Then he hoisted her into his arms. "Good."

He turned in the foyer, cutting across the oversize room, past the sofa, the armchair and television. He set her on her feet next to a king-size bed.

His hands went to his waistband, stripping off his pants and everything else.

She kicked off her sandals and dispensed with the panties.

She straightened, and they both stilled.

"You're beautiful," he whispered, and she felt the edge of her mouth draw into a smile.

"You're not so bad yourself." She dared to reach out, tracing her index finger along his smooth, warm chest. He looked even better out of his clothes than he had in them, and that was saying something.

He took a half step forward. "Is this a dream?"

"I sure hope not."

"Things like this. Things like you don't happen in real life."

"I'm real."

"You're amazing."

Impatient, she took his hand, backing her way to the bed, where she sank down.

His gaze stayed molten on her naked body as he extracted a packet from his wallet and dropped the wallet to the floor.

"I can make this slow," he offered again.

She shook her head. "You're my torrid one-night stand."

"Oh, sweetheart," he whispered.

She smiled saucily in return. This was the only time she was ever going to do this, and she was going to get it right. "Show me what you've got."

He cupped his hands beneath her arms, lifting her, pushing her farther onto the bed, laying her back. His voice was a deep baritone, rumbling through her. "Seriously. Where in the hell have you been all my life?"

She didn't have time to answer because his mouth came down on hers. His body covered her own, pressing her against the soft mattress.

He toured her body with rapid but thorough kisses, while she explored the contours and angles of his. Within minutes, they were face-to-face, him on top, staring into each other's eyes in the dimly lit room.

He flexed, and she moaned, welcoming him inside, arching her back, wrapping her legs, as he set an insistent rhythm that made her head tip back and her eyes close tight. Desire overwhelmed her, and she gripped the comforter, straining for his kisses, her toes curling as he inflamed the passion at her core.

Time lost all meaning. Her body felt somehow weightless. Reality contracted to the feel, the scent and the sound of this man. His ragged breath murmured in her ear. His damp body scorched her skin. And she dragged his essence into her lungs, holding it tight, imprinting it on her subconscious so she could relive it over and over again.

She held on as long as she could, not wanting it to end. But it was a losing battle. A pulse began deep inside her, building to a tidal wave of ecstasy. She clung tightly to him, her cries mingling with his groans, as she crested for an eternity, the intense rush leaving her limp and gasping.

Her chest rose and fell against Lucky's comfortable weight. He braced himself on his elbows, rising slightly above her, sweat glistening his brow, breath fanning from between his parted lips.

They stared at each other in silence.

"That was…" His breathless voice trailed away.

She was similarly struggling for words. "It was," she agreed.

His smile widened. "Somehow we both seem to know just the right thing to say."

A small chuckle formed in her chest. "What do you usually say?"

He smoothed her hair behind one ear. "I have no comparables. You have no comparables. You are one of a kind, Doll-Face."

"That was an awfully good line," she acknowledged.

"It wasn't a line."

They both fell silent, their breathing synchronizing.

His tone when low and intimate. "Should I ask if it was good for you?"

It was the best sex she'd ever had. Hands down.

Without waiting for an answer, he shifted, taking more of his own weight. "You want that wine now, or are you ready for breakfast?"

Abigail glanced to the digital clock glowing on the nightstand. It was four-thirty in the morning. She blinked against grainy exhaustion. "It's pretty much a toss-up between night and morning, isn't it?"

He eased onto his side, propping himself on his elbow, one thigh staying angled across her legs. He brushed a wisp of hair from her cheek. "I'd like it to still be night."

She drank in the sensation of that intimate touch. "I'd like it to still be dinner."

He eased closer. "So we can start our evening all over again?"

She pretended he might have it wrong. "Yeah. Sure. Well, that and the mountain burger."

Closer still, he brought his teeth gently down on her earlobe. "Liar."

"Egomaniac."

"Am I wrong?"

She played dumb. "About what?"

He glanced at the clock. "About us wanting to stop time."

She sobered. Then she shook her head. He wasn't wrong. But

that didn't change anything. "It's a stolen night," she reminded him. They both had places to go and things to do.

"When do you have to leave?"

"Early." She was meeting her brother at the campaign office to close things up before she drove back to the ranch.

Lucky cradled her cheek, placing a long, tender kiss on her swollen lips. When it ended, his arm eased around the small of her back. "But not yet?"

"Not yet," she agreed, desire rising inside her.

He kissed her again, and again, longer and sweeter each time.

"Tell me your name," he demanded.

She shook her head.

"I need to know." He drew back, obviously determined to withhold more kisses until she answered.

Instead, she reached up, slipping her arms around his neck.

He tensed against her pull, resisting, but then he gave in, allowing her to bring him in for a kiss. She twined her naked body around his.

"Oh, Doll-Face," he groaned, capitulating to their passion. He wrapped his strong arms fully around her, holding her close and igniting a new burn deep inside.

"There you are, Abby." Abigail's oldest brother, Seth, mayor-elect of Lyndon City, zeroed in on her as she entered the campaign office on Main Street.

Cardboard boxes covered every available surface, stuffed with leftover posters, flyers, buttons and campaign literature. Half a dozen campaign volunteers were carting boxes and other materials out the back door to waiting pickup trucks, while the staffers who would form the core of Seth's mayoral staff clicked away on their laptop computers or talked on telephones.

Seth tucked a pen into his shirt pocket as he moved across the storefront shop toward her. "I didn't see you at the fireworks last night."

"Weren't they great?" she asked, avoiding any further explanation of where she'd been.

"The good folks of Lyndon know how to do it up right," he agreed.

She gave him a quick hug. "The good folks of Lyndon are excited about their new mayor."

Seth pulled back with a grin. "The display was planned weeks before the votes were cast."

She winked at him. "But I'm sure they'd have canceled if you hadn't won."

He scoffed out a laugh. "Since we both know you're not naive, I'm going to assume that's blind loyalty talking."

"That's supreme confidence talking." She patted him on the shoulder as she glanced around the messy office. "You need any help here?" She was more than a little anxious to get herself out of town. Last night Lucky had said he was just passing through Lyndon. He might very well have left town already. But she didn't want to risk running into him.

She'd sneaked out of his hotel room and back to hers as soon as he fell asleep last night. Though the soft bed, the thick quilt and Lucky's warm, strong body had been powerful draws, she hadn't wanted to risk facing him in the morning. Better to leave things on a high note. A very high note. Wow, had that ever been a high note.

"Abby?" Seth prompted, waving his palm in front of her face.

"The financial records?"

"What about them?"

"What's the matter with you?"

"Nothing."

Seth peered at her curiously. "I just asked if you could do a double check on the donation receipts. And Lisa needs a hand with the database."

At the sound of her name, Lisa Thompson glanced up from a crowded desk in one corner of the room. "I want to make sure we have a clean backup copy before I delete all the information from the laptop. I'm planning to use it in the mayor's office, so I have to get rid of all the campaign records."

"Happy to help out," Abigail agreed, telling herself the odds of seeing Lucky were low, particularly if she was hidden away in the back of the campaign office. She made her way across the room, weaving around the mess of chairs, desks, boxes and trash bins.

Seth's cell phone rang, and he moved to a quiet corner near the back exit to answer the call.

Lisa, blonde, petite, freckled and perky, tracked Abigail's progress from her office chair.

She waited until Abigail sat down and spun the chair, then she wheeled herself to face her. "So, what happened?" she demanded in a conspiratorial undertone.

"What are you talking about?"

"It's blatantly obvious you got laid last night."

"What?" Abigail blurted, glancing swiftly around, making sure nobody could overhear them.

"Don't play dumb with me." Lisa smacked her palm down on the padded arm of Abigail's chair.

"I did not—"

"And don't you dare lie to me either." Lisa rocked back and crossed her arms over her gray Colorado Lions T-shirt, green eyes narrowing. Her voice stayed low. "Your cheeks are flushed. Your eyes are glowing gold. And there's a spring in your step that wasn't there at the party. Plus, you disappeared before ten last night, and I never saw you again. Neither did anyone else. Now, give."

Abigail hesitated. She wanted to lie, but she knew she was trapped. Lisa had her dead to rights.

Obviously taking Abigail's silence as an admission, Lisa grinned and leaned closer still. "Details, please."

Abigail sent a worried glance toward Seth. "Don't you dare tell—"

"I'm not going to tell anybody. I'm not a gossip."

Abigail knew it was true. Lisa would be Seth's executive assistant in the mayor's office, in part because of her brilliance and hard work, but also because they'd learned she was the soul of discretion. She and Abigail had become quite close over the course of the campaign.

"So, what happened?" Lisa hissed. "Who was he?"

"Nobody you know."

"How can you say that? I know lots of people. I've met half the town in the last three months."

"He's not from here."

"Ooh." Lisa's eyes sparkled. "Where's he from? What's he do? What's his name? Is he hot?"

"I don't know."

Lisa drew back. "You don't know if he's hot?"

"I don't know his name," Abigail admitted sheepishly. "I don't know what he does. And I don't know where he's from."

Lisa's mouth opened, then her expression turned positively gleeful. "You had a one-night stand with a stranger?"

Abigail lowered her own voice even further. "Yes."

Lisa's hand tightened on Abigail's arm, as if to hold her in place. "Was he hot?"

"Yes." Hot didn't begin to describe Lucky. In fact, even now, Abigail's body responded with an embarrassing level of arousal at the mere memory of Lucky naked, laconic, gazing at her with that lazy half smile.

"You go, Abby!"

"Shh."

"Yes. Of course. Wow. No wonder you don't want to tell Seth."

"I don't want to tell *anyone*."

Lisa gave a series of rapid nods. "Got it. But if you don't know his name, how are you going to see him again?"

"I'm not." Abigail wouldn't. She couldn't. No matter how much she wished she could.

"But if he's hot and, well, if the look in your eyes is anything to go by, maybe you want to—"

"Lisa, look up the definition of one-night stand."

"One-night stands can turn into something else, you know."

Abigail coughed on a laugh, seizing on the chance to turn the tables. "Actually, I wouldn't know. Would you?"

Lisa wrinkled her nose in the air. "No. Not that there's anything wrong in it. Not with the right person. You know, in the right circumstance."

"Last night was the right circumstance." Abigail wasn't going to regret last night. She refused to regret last night.

She'd never met a man remotely like Lucky. The memory of his voice made her tingle, and the thought of his kisses brought a flood of desire. Her real world was closing in fast, dragging her back into its clutches, while the exhilarating escape with Lucky secretly pulsed just below her skin. She'd lock it away where no one could see, but where she could pull it out to relive that treasured night over and over again.

Fall was on its way to Lyndon Valley. Work on the ranch would begin in earnest now, starting with the roundup. But when the wind howled down from the Rockies, or when she was bone tired out on the range, she'd remember the feel of Lucky's strong arms around her, the heat of his body against her, his whispered words, his endearing sense of humor and the way he'd made her feel like the only woman in the world.

Three

The Craig Mountain Brewery was tucked in the mountains above the picturesque shores of Lake Patricia, an hour north of Lyndon City. Built of stone and mortar, around 1850, in the style of British castles, Craig Mountain had started life as a manor house for a British lord, a remittance man, a reprobate whose family had paid him handsomely to leave England and never return.

The brewery manager, Lucas Payton, shared the story of Lord Ashton with Zach while the two men made their way along the covered pathway that connected the original castle, which was now mostly offices, to the newer industrial complex housing the warehouse and brewery, with its tanks, filtration systems and bottling line.

"They say Ashton bribed a railroad official for information on the planned railway line," Lucas continued, tone animated. "Whether the official didn't know the real route, or he simply lied for reasons of his own, nobody ever found out. But he took the money and left the state, while Ashton built his house a hundred miles in the wrong direction."

"You a history buff?" asked Zach.

Lucas had worked for DFB for three years now. The two men

had met on several occasions when Lucas traveled to Houston for company meetings. But they'd always talked shop, and it had always been amongst a larger group of people.

"You know how it is," Lucas answered, stuffing his hands into his back pockets. "I'm an orphan. So I've adopted somebody's else's ancestors."

"Never thought to do that," said Zach. Interesting, though, choosing a family history based on interest and convenience instead of strict genealogy.

Like all DFB employees, Lucas had come through the foster care system. When Zach and Alex founded the company, they'd promised each other it would be for the benefit of orphans like themselves, people who had no families and few chances in life.

"You should prowl through the top floors of the castle sometime," said Lucas, pulling open a door to the cinder-block warehouse. "There's some absolutely fascinating stuff up there."

"I'm not going to have time for that." Zach stepped inside the cool, dim building, and the familiar tang of hops and malt hit his nostrils. Supplies were stacked twenty feet high on steel shelving, on either side of a wide aisle that bisected the big building. A forklift rumbled unseen in the distance, its backup alarm sounding intermittently with the whir of the tires and hydraulics.

"Going right back to the big city?" asked Lucas. "I suppose there's not much to keep you here."

"Not much," Zach agreed, even as his mind slipped back to last night and the incredible encounter with Doll-Face.

When he woke up this morning, the sexy and mysterious woman had already slipped out, leaving him there alone. He'd told himself to let it go. She didn't want to know him, and she sure hadn't wanted him to know anything about her.

It was disappointing, and for a few seconds he'd been tempted to hang around town looking for her. But orphans learned one lesson very early in life. Anything good could be snatched away in a millisecond. It was probably better that it had happened fast this time. Something told him, given half a chance, he could have fallen dangerously hard for the beautiful, intelligent, engaging woman.

He came back to the present as Lucas started through the center of the warehouse.

"It's not the renovation costs that'll get you," said Lucas, turning the conversation back to the reason for Zach's visit. "And there's plenty of room to expand out back toward the hillside."

He pressed a red button on the wall, and a big overhead door clattered its way open. He pointed outside to the vast gravel parking lot, past two semitrailer trucks that were positioned for unloading. "We can build a new warehouse over there, free up some space for more production. The bottling plant and the brewery will have to stay put, but we'd have some options around the coolers and the fermenters."

"If it's not the renovation costs, what is it that'll get me?" asked Zach, used to cutting directly to the chase.

"The water," said Lucas.

"Something wrong with the water?"

"We've maxed out the water license. I asked around after your call on Friday, and it's going to be tough, if not impossible, to get permission to increase our usage."

This was very bad news. Zach frowned. "Why?"

"Moratorium on water-use licenses all across the region."

The unique underground springwater of Craig Mountain was a key ingredient in the beer. The springwater was also the cornerstone of the marketing campaign for C Mountain Ale, the most popular brand in DFB's iconic Red, White and Brew six-pack.

Red, White and Brew contained one beer from each of DFB's six breweries, and it was taking their international markets by storm. Production was already on pace for the new orders at the other five breweries in Montana, California, Michigan, South Carolina and Texas, but Craig Mountain had to catch up.

"The water-rights battle has been going on for months. It's the ranchers versus everyone else, and the ranchers are a very powerful lobby group."

"We're miles and miles from the nearest ranch." Zach gestured through the big doorway. "How can our water use possibly impact them?"

"It doesn't matter," said Lucas, shaking his head. "People have grazing rights nearby. There'll be no new water licenses. No variances to existing water licenses. No temporary permits. Nothing until the new regulations are drafted and they go through the state legislature."

Zach swore.

"You got that right."

Zach smacked the heel of his hand against the doorjamb. He gritted his teeth. Then he straightened and squared his shoulders. "All right. Who do I talk to?"

"Beats the hell out of me. I do beer, not politics."

"Well, who does politics?"

"You could try a lawyer. Someone local, maybe."

Zach nodded. He supposed that was a logical place to start. "Who do you use locally?"

Lucas gave a shrug. "We've never had any legal problems."

"Are there law firms in Lyndon?"

Or maybe he should fly back to Denver. If this moratorium thing was broader than the immediate Lyndon area, he might as well go to a big firm with plenty of capacity.

And his clock was ticking. If the Craig Mountain Brewery construction didn't get started in the next couple of weeks, they'd end up with a shortage of C Mountain Ale, and they wouldn't be able to fill their spring orders for Red, White and Brew. That would most certainly mean the downfall of DFB.

"There are definitely law firms in Lyndon." Lucas answered the question. "Sole proprietorships mostly. And I don't know if they've been involved in the issue. Honestly, if I was going for the greatest concentration of knowledge on this, I'd be going to the Ranchers Association."

"Didn't you just say they were on the other side?"

"I did."

"So, then, that would be a foolish move."

"Well." Lucas scratched the back of his neck. "If you don't

want to go to the Ranchers Association, you can try Abigail Jacobs."

"Who's she?"

"The daughter of one of the ranching families. I was told she has an encyclopedia for a brain and a passion for the water-rights issue."

"She's still the enemy."

"Maybe. Technically."

"So she's not going to help us."

"You can always get creative. You don't have to tell her exactly what you're looking for. Just meet her and, I don't know." Lucas looked Zach up and down. "Tell her she's pretty or something, take her out for dinner and a movie, then ask a lot of questions."

"You want me to romance the information out of some unsuspecting woman?"

"If she's a research geek, maybe she hasn't had a date for a while."

"Did we not give you an ethics quiz before we hired you?"

"I had a dysfunctional upbringing."

"So did I, but I still have standards. I'm going with the lawyer." The clock might be ticking, but Zach had absolutely no intention of lying to this Abigail Jacobs for his own ends.

The Jacobs ranch covered thousands of acres in the Lyndon Valley of western Colorado. As it had become more prosperous, Abigail's grandfather, and then her father, had purchased more and more land. The main house was two stories high, with six bedrooms, overlooking the Lyndon River to the east. To the west the Rockies rose, their peaks jutting to the blue sky behind the three main barns, several horse corrals and a massive equipment garage.

Staff cottages and two low bunkhouses snaked along the riverbank, forming a semicircle around the big cookshack that welcomed cowboys and farmhands with wholesome food and pots of brewed coffee any time of the day or night. Born and raised here, Abigail knew there were many things to love about the

Jacobs ranch, and she now spent her days reminding herself she could be happy here. She climbed the front stairs, the summer day's sweat soaking through her T-shirt, dampening her hairline and wicking into the band of her Stetson. As she started across the porch, she heard male voices through the open living-room windows. The sun was slipping low in the hot August sky. The breeze had dropped to nothing. And a dozen horseflies buzzed a lazy patrol pattern beneath the shade of the peaked porch roof. She slapped her hat against her leg, brushed the excess dust from the front of her jeans, then checked her boot heels for mud.

The voices grew louder, more distinct. One was her brother Travis. The other was vaguely familiar, but she couldn't quite place it.

"And you expect *us* to help?" Travis demanded.

"I could have lied," the other voice returned reasonably. "But in the interest of—"

"Is that supposed to impress me? That you stopped short of lying?"

"I'm not looking to impress you."

Wondering who her brother was arguing with, Abigail moved toward the door. In the week since she'd returned to the ranch, there'd been a steady stream of friends and neighbors stopping by, expressing their congratulations on Seth's victory and inquiring about Abigail's father, who was expected home from the Houston rehab center in the next few weeks.

"Lucky for you that you're not," scoffed Travis.

"I just want some information, and then I'll be on my—"

"You'll be on your way right now."

"Not before I talk to Abigail."

Abigail stopped short. Who *was* that?

"Abigail's not here."

"Then I'll wait."

"I don't think so."

Well, whoever it was, he wasn't going to have to wait long, and it was going to be a pretty short conversation. Abigail had a hot shower in her sights, followed by dinner and maybe a nice glass of Shiraz. Then she was falling directly into bed.

She wasn't exactly out of shape, but it had been several months since she'd done full-time ranch work, and her long shift on the oat field today had been exhausting.

"Nobody gets to Abby unless they go through me," Travis stated.

From the entry hall, Abigail could picture her brother's square shoulders, his wide stance, the hard line of his chin. He was endearingly, if unnecessarily, protective. She pushed down the door latch with her thumb and silently opened the door.

The unknown man's voice came from around the corner, inside the big living room. "Craig Mountain's new usage will be negligible in the scheme of things."

"And what better way to set precedent?" Travis responded. "You're the thin edge of the wedge."

"I'm brewing beer, not setting precedent. It's one little underground spring."

"It's still part of the aquifer."

Abigail dropped her hat on a peg by the door and raked back her damp, dusty hair. Her ponytail was definitely the worse for wear. Then again, so were her dirty hands and her sweaty clothes. But she was back on the ranch now. And she wasn't looking to impress anyone. So who cared?

During the local-water-rights hearings a few months ago, she'd listened to every argument in the book. It wouldn't take her long to send this guy packing.

She rounded the corner. "Hey, Travis."

Her brother scowled.

The broad-shouldered man in the expensive business suit pivoted to face her.

As he did, she went stock-still. Her stomach plummeted to her toes, while waves of sound roared in her ears. *"Lucky?"*

His dark eyes widened.

"Lucky what?" asked Travis, glancing from one to the other.

Abigail's brain stumbled, and an exaggerated second slipped by. "Lucky I got here when I did," she managed to say on a hollow laugh.

Where on earth had he come from? What was he doing standing here arguing with her brother?

Before she could formulate any kind of question, Lucky stepped forward, holding out his hand. "Zach Rainer. You must be Abigail. It's nice to meet you."

"Mr. Rainer was just leaving," Travis put in with finality.

"I own the Craig Mountain Brewery," Zach continued, his voice betraying none of the recognition evident in his expression.

"I...uh..." Her throat closed over. "I'm Abigail," she managed to rasp, giving his hand a perfunctory shake. The sizzle of his brief touch ricocheted up her arm.

"Then you're the woman I'm here to see. I understand you have some expertise on the regional-water-rights issue."

Travis stepped forward. "Oh, no, you don't."

"I'd like to talk to Abigail."

"But Abigail wouldn't like to talk to you."

"I think Abigail can speak for herself." Lucky raised his brow.

She struggled to shake off the shock. So far, he was keeping their night a secret. Although she had to find out what he was up to, and quickly.

"It's okay, Travis," she said with a quick glance to her brother.

"No, it's not okay. He doesn't get to waltz in here and—"

"I'm not out to harm you." Though Lucky was responding to Travis, he kept his gaze fixed on Abigail.

"You're a liar," said Travis.

Abigail agreed with her brother. Lucky's being here couldn't possibly be a coincidence. Had he set her up from the very beginning? A wave of disappointment and humiliation washed over her.

"I'm not lying," said Lucky.

The odds were overwhelming that he was lying through his teeth, but one thing was sure, she needed to talk to him alone. Bad enough that she'd slept with him, but in the wee hours of the morning she'd also confessed embarrassing secrets. She'd told him how badly she wanted a career in business, that she didn't want to work with her brother on the ranch. She'd said some things that, in retrospect, were downright disloyal.

"It'll be fine," she assured Travis in the calmest voice she could muster.

"You don't need to be polite," Travis pointed out. "This guy's the enemy."

Lucky heaved a frustrated sigh.

"I'm a grown woman." Abigail was firm. "I think I can decide who to talk to."

"Don't start with me," said Travis.

"Can we step outside?" asked Lucky, taking a step toward the door.

Travis barged between the two, facing Lucky, his back to Abigail. "Leave," he commanded.

"Travis," she said from between clenched teeth. "You have to back off."

"No."

"We're only going to talk."

He rounded on her. "I don't understand. Why would you give this jerk the time of day?"

"I'm giving him five minutes."

Travis spread his arms in obvious frustration. "I've already given him ten."

Fine, Abigail was frustrated, too. When Travis got like this, there was no point in arguing with him. But she didn't dare give in, not until she knew what Lucky was up to. She held her palms up in surrender and took a backward step, then another, and another.

When she was clear, she turned for the door, stomping her way outside, assuming Lucky—no, *Zach*—would have sense enough to follow. Her brother was a tough, intimidating man. But Zach seemed as if he could hold his own. And she was hoping against hope they were too civilized to engaged in a fistfight in the living room.

She banged her way through the front doorway, stomped across the porch, down onto the gravel driveway, taking a few steps out onto the turnaround. She pushed back her hair, acutely aware of her disheveled appearance.

She shouldn't care. But she couldn't seem to help herself. Zach had seen her at her best last week, dressed up for the party. Okay, so he'd also seen her naked. But she didn't think she looked that bad naked.

Right now her shirt was wrinkled and covered in grit. She was pretty sure there were dust streaks marring her face. Her hair looked like something out of a horror flick. And she smelled like the rear end of a heifer.

"Abigail?" came Zach's voice, followed by his swift footsteps crunching on the gravel.

She squared her shoulders and turned to face him.

"What are you doing here?" she asked shortly.

"I need your help." He came to a halt a few feet away.

"No. I mean, *what are you doing here?*"

"I don't get the distinction."

"How did you find me? Did you know who I was all along?" She feared she already knew the answer, but she wanted him to admit it out loud.

"I didn't find you. I didn't even know who you were."

"Right," she scoffed. He had to have targeted her from minute one. She could only imagine he'd been laughing at her all night long.

"I didn't know your name," he insisted with remarkable sincerity. "I met Doll-Face. I *liked* Doll-Face." He paused, and an emotion flicked through his eyes. "Why wouldn't you tell me your name?"

"Apparently I didn't need to."

"I didn't know your name," he repeated. "It was only *later* I heard that Abigail Jacobs was the best person to help me with the water license. I put those two things together exactly two minutes ago."

"You expect me to believe that?" Had she come across as completely stupid and gullible? What a depressing thought.

"Yes, I expect you to believe me."

"I believed you were leaving town," she challenged. "That was a week ago, Zach. You haven't left town."

"I told you I was passing through."

"What kind of play on semantics is that?"

"I *am* passing through."

"You set me up from the start." There was no other explanation.

He spread his legs, firming his stance. "I did not know who you were that night."

"Bull."

"I didn't. If I had…" He paused. "Hell, I don't know what I would have done if I had. That night was pretty great."

"You don't get to talk about that night." Not now, not ever.

"It doesn't matter if I talk about it or not." His gaze smoldered for a silent second, transmitting the unspoken message that he remembered it as well as she did.

"It's nothing more than a blur to me," she bluffed.

He eased closer. "You can't lie worth a damn."

"Yes, I can." The protest was reflexive. She didn't want to be a good liar, and his opinion meant nothing to her.

"I need your help, Doll-Face."

She leaned in, pointing an index finger at his chest. "You can't have my help."

"Oh, I'm pretty sure I can." His tone was mild, but his eyes had gone hard as flint.

A cloud moved over the setting sun, cooling the air and darkening the world, while a sick feeling settled in the pit of her stomach.

"I saw your look of panic inside the house," he finished.

"That wasn't panic," she lied again.

"You don't want your brother to know about us," Zach stated.

As if on cue, Travis appeared in the doorway, leaning on the jamb, arms folded over his chest and a scowl on his face.

Abigail didn't dare let Zach know he had the upper hand. "Believe me when I tell you, *you* don't want my brothers to know about us."

"I'll take my chances with your brothers."

Did she dare call his bluff? Was it a bluff? Was he willing to risk her brothers' wrath over a water license? Her skin prickled and her heart rate doubled.

Okay, this might be the beginning of panic.

"I am certain," he continued, voice lower, leaning ever so slightly toward her, "that you want to keep every damn thing we said and did that night a secret."

She refused to answer.

"And that gives me a whole lot of bargaining power."

"Are you blackmailing me?" she demanded.

"Yeah," he admitted. Again, something flickered across his face. It could have been regret, but that seemed unlikely. "Sorry about that. But I'm in a hurry, and I need your brain."

"Was that supposed to be a joke?" she demanded, arms reflexively crossing over her breasts.

"What joke?"

"That you've already had my body?"

"I never said that."

"You thought it."

"You're paranoid."

She swallowed convulsively, attempting to moisten her throat. "How can you do this to me?"

"I wish I had a choice."

"You have a choice," she rasped. "You can walk away right now and forget any of this ever happened."

He crossed his arms over his broad chest. "Forget about today or forget about that night?"

"Go to hell."

Zach didn't flinch.

Travis stalked out onto the porch, and she knew he was about to intervene. He couldn't break this up. Not yet. Not until she convinced Zach to go away and never come back.

"Follow me," she told Zach, turning for the path that led to the river.

With a glance at Travis, Zach fell into step. "Is he going to let us leave?"

"Fifty-fifty," she allowed, wondering the same thing herself.

They cut off the edge of the driveway, moving onto the narrower path, where willows would partially screen them from Travis's view. She took a surreptitious glance over her shoulder, making sure her brother wasn't following.

"It's not like I'm asking you to knock over a bank," said Zach.

"You're asking me to betray my community."

"Don't be melodramatic. Nobody even has to know you're helping me. It'll be a secret."

"So you can blackmail me with it later?" she challenged.

He gave an exaggerated eye roll. "Don't be ridiculous."

"How is that ridiculous? You're blackmailing me now." Her voice came out more shrilly than she'd intended.

"There's only one thing I want from you, Abby."

"Don't call me Abby." That nickname was reserved for her family.

"I like it."

"You don't get to like it."

His gaze stayed on her, while he obviously regrouped. "How can we make this work?"

"You can go away and never come back."

"I'm definitely not going away. I need a variance on my water license. Nothing more, nothing less. Hundreds of jobs depend on it. And from everything I've learned in the last week, you're the only person who can help."

"I'll email you my research," she offered out of desperation.

"I need more than your research. I need to know who to ask, what to ask them, how to write the application and how to fight my way through the bureaucracy."

"My brain is not for sale."

"Yeah? Well, when it comes to my employees, my morals and values are open to the highest bidder." Passion and determination moved into his tone. "Don't push me, Abby. I'll do anything, *anything* to keep them from losing their jobs."

"If I help you set a precedent for varying a nonranching water license, my family's cause gets set back by miles."

"You'll have to gain the ground back later."

"You couldn't care less about me, could you?"

He didn't answer.

Then again, maybe he did. His silence said it all.

She clamped her jaw against her anger, realizing there was nothing left to say, no argument she could make that would change his mind. Zach had given her an impossible choice. She could be secretly disloyal, or blatantly disloyal.

If she was blatantly disloyal, there was no going back. If she secretly helped Zach, maybe, just maybe, the fallout would be manageable. At least she'd know the ins and outs of his strategy for getting around the water license. Maybe she could use that later, in some kind of political counterattack. Maybe.

"Well?" he prompted, and she knew her time was up.

"Fine," she ground out, accepting that she was trapped. "I'll do this for you. But if you ever dare tell my family anything—" she lifted her index finger, jabbing it against his chest "—and I mean anything about *anything,* I swear I will hunt you down and shoot you dead."

"Not a word," he vowed.

She paused, shaking off the sick feeling of disloyalty. "We can't talk here." And meeting in town was also a risk, with Seth and his staff all there.

"Come out to the brewery," Zach suggested.

It wasn't her first choice. But at least it was out of the way.

"It'll take me a couple of days to pull things together," she told him. "And I'll need to come up with an excuse to leave the ranch." She'd only just returned home to help Travis. It was going to take some fast talking to get away again. And she'd be leaving all the work to him. "I hate this."

"I'm not crazy about it either." Zach's eyes unexpectedly softened. His lips parted. A breeze washed over them, rustling the leaves.

He reached out, grazing the top of her hand with his. "You know, I really wish we could—"

"Don't," she warned him, darting away, even as her pulse leaped at his light touch. "Don't you dare try anything. I am *not* going to sleep with the man who's blackmailing me."

He dropped his hand. Then he blinked his expression back to neutral. He gave a sharp nod of acceptance. "Of course you're not. The brewery, then. Thursday morning. Be there."

Four

As she turned onto the Craig Mountain Brewery road, a Sawyer Brown tune came through the stereo speakers, and Abigail cranked up the volume, letting the beat pound its way through her brain. After she'd lied to her brother Travis this morning about where she was going, she'd promised herself she'd give Zach one day. She'd work fast. She'd work hard. And he'd have everything he needed to apply for his license.

Then she'd spend the night in Lyndon, head back to the ranch and forget she'd ever met the man.

Her plan to fantasize about him had come to an abrupt end when she'd learned that he had no scruples. Okay, maybe the end wasn't quite so abrupt. In fact, she was still working on it. It turned out that fantasizing about Zach was a hard habit to break. Which only made her hate him more.

How dare he mess up her life like this? It was a mere one-night stand. Was she not entitled to cut loose and have fun every once in a while? Thousands of women across the country had one-night stands. She was willing to bet things like this didn't happen to them.

Then again, she supposed they hadn't slept with Zach.

It would have been easier if she could just plain hate him. But he'd been such a perfect lover, she couldn't help wishing for the fantasy. If she could have Lucky back, she'd be looking forward to today.

They'd talk and joke and flirt, maybe kiss a little, maybe even cancel her reservation at Rose Cottages....

Whoa. She abruptly pulled back on that thought. She wrestled her imagination into submission as she navigated a series of potholes. Then she rounded a corner, and the massive stone castle of Craig Mountain rose in front of her. She rocked to a halt in the parking lot, fingers going white as she gripped the steering wheel.

The band had changed songs, belting out one about the winner losing it all. Abigail didn't particularly feel like a winner, but the rest fit. Her pride had been battered and bruised, and if she dared let her anger slip out of place, her emotions felt a whole lot like heartache.

Zach greeted Abigail in the brewery's reception area, which was once a foyer to the massive, stone castle. She was glaring at him, displeasure palpable in her flashing golden eyes. She wore torn, faded blue jeans, a powder-blue cotton shirt with the sleeves rolled halfway up her forearms, the top button missing, and a pair of battered cowboy boots, with a gray backpack slung over one shoulder. Her face was scrubbed free of makeup, and her glossy auburn hair was pulled back in a plain ponytail. She couldn't have telegraphed "don't touch me" any louder if she'd shouted it from the highest tower.

He knew she thought he'd set her up. He hadn't. But there was no way to make her believe it. Too bad. Because whatever it was that had attracted him that night wasn't going away anytime soon. She could dress down all she liked. She was still off-the-charts sexy in his eyes.

"Good morning," he offered.

"Morning," she returned, stony faced.

"Thanks for coming."

She scoffed and shrugged her shoulders. "Like I had a choice. Tell me what you need, and let's get this over with."

Zach couldn't help a surreptitious glance at the receptionist stationed at the counter across the room, trying to gauge if she was within earshot. It seemed unlikely, but there was no point in taking chances.

"You want the tour first?" he asked Abigail, using an outstretched arm to direct her toward the main door.

Craig Mountain Brewery offered tours of the castle, the facilities and the grounds. According to Lucas, there were quite a few tourists willing to make the hour-long, scenic drive to visit a historic castle and sample Craig Mountain beer. At the last managers' meeting in Houston, Zach and Alex had turned down Lucas's proposal to put in a small restaurant. But Zach was now rethinking that decision.

"Why would I want a tour?" Abigail asked without moving.

"Because it's interesting."

She crossed her arms mulishly over her chest. "I'm not here to see the sights."

In his peripheral vision, he saw the receptionist move to the far side of the cavernous room. Nice to know the staff were courteous.

"I need you to understand how we operate here. How else are you going to argue our case?"

"I'm not arguing your case. I'm giving you some information. What you do with it is entirely up to you."

"That wasn't our deal."

"We don't have a deal. We have a blackmail scheme."

True enough. "You're being melodramatic again."

She jabbed a thumb over her shoulder. "Then I can walk back out that door and not worry about any negative repercussions?"

"No, you can't," he admitted.

"I rest my case."

"See, you're good at this."

She frowned. "You expect me to laugh?"

"I expect you to let me show you around Craig Mountain Brewery." He gestured toward the door again.

She gave a hard, exaggerated sigh and hiked up the backpack. "If that's what'll get this over and done with."

"That's what'll get this over and done with," he confirmed.

She lifted her nose in the air, pivoted on those scuffed boots and marched for the door.

He couldn't help watching her rear end as she walked away. The woman had the sexiest body he'd ever seen. He supposed that's what happened when you combined natural beauty, fresh air and healthy living. The hot got hotter.

Abigail was scorching.

He followed her outside to where semicircular, stone steps led to a gravel parking lot. They were bordered by the castle lawns on the lake side and by forests of maples, aspens and evergreen trees stretching up the hill on the other. As August wound to a close, the barest hint of changing leaves had appeared. Beyond the tree line, the mountains turned to scrub and then craggy rock.

The expanse of green lawn stretched toward a rocky cliff that dropped to Lake Patricia. At the cliff's edge was a massive statue of Lord Ashton, chest puffed out, sword drawn, perched on a magnificent charger that seemed to gallop toward the water.

Zach had to admit, if it wasn't for the worry about DFB's future and the discord with Abigail, he would have enjoyed his stay here. He'd taken a small but very comfortable suite on the third floor of the castle. He'd even poked his head up to the small, dusty, rotund turrets. Lucas was right, the castle was a treasure trove of memorabilia.

"That's the statue of Lord Ashton," Zach offered as an opening.

"Is he currently brewing beer?" Abigail tartly inquired.

"He is not."

"Then I don't need to know about him." She rounded on Zach. "Can we move it along? Let's stick to the things I need to know."

Zach couldn't really blame her for being testy. And blackmailing her wasn't exactly his most admirable undertaking. But life was tough. You took your advantages where you could. And in a few days, she'd be finished with him, and she'd be back in the bosom of her family, doing the ranch job she hated, none the worse for wear.

Come to think of it. She should be grateful to him for giving her a reprieve from roping and riding and branding. He wondered if he'd be able to make her see it that way, or at least get her to admit that he wasn't dragging her to the gallows. Helping Craig Mountain get a few thousand more gallons of water each day wasn't going to fundamentally change anything, except the lives of Zach's employees. And that would be for the good.

"The brewery's down this path," he offered, nodding the way.

She reluctantly fell into step beside him. "And I need to see it why?"

"We brew C Mountain Ale up here," Zach began. "It's Craig Mountain's signature product, and its unique taste comes, in part, from the local, underground springwater." They rounded a corner of the path, and the gray, industrial complex came into view. "Nationwide and worldwide, hundreds of microbreweries are going under in today's economy. We're in danger of joining them, except that we have one product that's taking our national and international markets by storm. Our Red, White and Brew six-pack."

"Red, White and Brew?"

"Very patriotic packaging. Consumers love it. It contains one beer from each of our breweries. They're in six different states. All the other facilities can keep up with the increased demand. But we need to triple production of C Mountain Ale."

"Why not replace C Mountain Ale with another beer?" she reasoned.

"Because it's one of the most popular in the pack. When you find the X factor in the beer business, in any business, you don't mess with it."

"Find another water source. It's water, Lucky. Water."

"From where?" He stopped and gestured around them. "From the lake? The river? Surface water is vastly different in chemical composition. It would need a different treatment. The taste would change. And—and this is the most important point—I'd have to get the bloody water license to do that anyway."

She didn't seem to have an answer for that.

"Do you have any idea how hard it is to hit on the exact formula for a popular beer?" he continued.

"Do you know how hard it is to lie to your family?"

"No," he stated flatly. "I don't."

They stared at each other in charged silence.

"Then why are you making me do it?"

Zach's heart contracted, and he was forced to push down an unfamiliar feeling of guilt. "I'm not. You can tell your family anything you want."

"If I'd told them the truth, I wouldn't be here."

"And your secret's safe with me."

"My conscience isn't."

"Your conscience will get over it." People had to do what they had to do in this life. It was a tiny bit of white lie, one of omission really. Zach had done far worse, and his conscience was perfectly clear.

"I'm going to hate you, Zach," she warned.

"I guess I'm going to have to find a way to live with that."

"You couldn't care less, could you?"

"No. I could care a whole lot less than I do." Truth was, he cared far more than he should. But his duty was to Alex and to his employees. He had to stay tough. He couldn't let his personal feelings for Abigail get in the way.

Abigail tried very hard not to show an interest in the inner workings of the brewery. But the manager made the tour quite fascinating, and she found herself impressed by the scope of the operation.

"The bottling plant—" wearing a hat and safety glasses, Lucas projected his voice over the rumble of the motors, the whir of the conveyors and the clatter of the bottles running past them toward the filling station "—is the one place we won't need any kind of upgrade. It's currently only operating at eighteen percent capacity, so there's plenty of room for growth. Good call on that when you bought it." He tipped his head to Zach.

Zach nodded an acknowledgment of the compliment but

didn't offer a response over the din. They bypassed the labeling conveyor to go through a swinging doorway, shutting out much of the noise. Then they headed down a short hallway that seemed to be leading them back to the warehouse.

Halfway down the hall, Lucas opened a door to a large, dimly lit room. It was lined with banks of computers, monitors and electrical panels that featured a host of blinking lights. "This is the nerve center of the operation."

Just then, Zach's cell phone rang. He peeled off the hat and safety glasses they'd been issued for the brewery leg of the tour, excusing himself to move farther down the hall.

Abigail removed her own hat and glasses, handing them to Lucas as they moved farther into the control room. Two staff members were walking from station to station, noting numbers and turning dials.

"We can monitor temperature, humidity, production, supplies and shipping," said Lucas. "You name it."

"Are all of the DFB breweries this big?" Abigail found herself asking.

"Craig Mountain is the smallest," Lucas replied. "But we've had some of the most recent upgrades, so we like to think we can hold our own."

"I'm sure you can. I have to say, I'm very impressed." The place seemed high-tech and very well run.

Lucas rested his butt against the edge of one of the long, black-topped counters. "And I have to say it's nice of you to help us out with this."

She retied her ponytail, compressing her lips. She had no intention of discussing the sordid details, but she wasn't willing to tell an outright lie. "Helping Craig Mountain wasn't my choice," she admitted.

He cocked his head. "I have to admit, I was surprised to hear that you'd said yes."

She tried to guess how much he knew about the blackmail. He seemed to be seeking information.

"Was it out of pity?" he probed.

"I'd call it insanity," she responded. "If Seth or Travis find out I'm doing this—"

Lucas came upright. "Wait a minute. Your brothers don't know you're here?"

Abigail stilled, a sinking feeling creeping into her stomach. "Zach didn't tell you to keep this a secret?"

"You helping us is a secret?"

"Yes."

"Are you kidding me?"

Abigail shook her head. Then she swallowed. Oh, no.

Lucas slipped an arm through hers. With a surreptitious glance at the two employees over his shoulder, he propelled her out the door and into the hallway. There, they all but ran into Zach.

"Please tell me there's more to this plan," Lucas opened, staring accusingly at his boss.

Zach moved his confused gaze from Lucas to Abigail and back again. "What plan?"

"She's *known,* Zach. She's recognizable."

Zach didn't respond, taking a moment to tuck his phone back into his pocket.

Lucas wasn't finished. "How in the hell is she going to explain being here?"

Zach's jaw went tight in obvious annoyance at Lucas's manner. "The details are none of your business."

"This brewery is my business," Lucas returned.

"Let's discuss this in private," Zach ground out.

But Lucas shook his head. "Fire me if you want to, but this isn't Houston or Denver. She's the mayor's sister. She has no anonymity. We need to get her out of here before people start asking questions."

Abigail knew with a sickening certainty that Lucas was right. When she agreed to meet Zach up here, she hadn't realized so many people worked at Craig Mountain. Most of them probably lived in Lyndon. She could only hope her hat and glasses had kept her from being recognized on the tour. But she was playing with fire, and she needed to get out of here.

"Everything we need to work with is in the offices," Zach pointed out. "She has to do it here."

"Well, it can't be during business hours. Bring her back later, preferably in the middle of the night. And put her in a disguise of some kind."

"I'm standing right here," Abigail couldn't help interjecting. Both men glanced at her.

"You're talking about me as if I'm not," she pointed out, feeling miffed.

"Sorry," said Lucas.

"You don't think a disguise is overkill?" Zach asked Lucas.

Lucas raised a brow to Abigail. "What do you think?"

"I think I was stupid to come here." She glanced from one to the other. "And so, having enjoyed a nice brewery tour, I'll take my leave."

"You still have work to do," Zach insisted.

"She needs to leave." Lucas backed her up.

"Then be here tonight," said Zach. "The second shift ends at ten. After that, nobody'll be here but security."

"Maybe wear a blond wig," Lucas put in.

"I'll phone you later," she told Zach, anxious to make herself scarce. She should have realized the danger. She definitely wasn't cut out for covert operations.

"You'll *come back* later," he insisted.

"It's too dangerous."

"Nobody will see you."

"You can't guarantee that."

"I'll make sure nobody sees you."

"Zach—"

"Abigail."

They gazed at each other for a long minute. Abigail knew a stubborn man when she saw one, and Zach was surely one of them.

"Tonight," he repeated. "The sooner we get our water license, the sooner you're off the hook."

She hated to admit he was right. But he was. The faster she learned about his business and showed him how to do his research and fill out the application form, the sooner he'd leave her alone. There wasn't a single chance they'd succeed, but he'd be forced to admit she tried.

Annoyed by the delay, but knowing she had no choice, Abigail headed into Lyndon for the afternoon. There, she took pity on herself and decided to go for a manicure at the Crystal Pool spa. Discovering they were having a three-treatments-for-the-price-of-two sale, she also had a facial and a wax job. Then she stopped by her favorite clothing store and picked up a pair of black jeans and a sleeveless, shimmering, royal-blue blouse with lace insets and a mandarin collar. The jeans were too long to go with her cowboy boots, and she found a kicky pair of rhinestone-decorated, high-heeled sandals to complete the look.

Afterward, she felt better, confident, more like herself. She checked into the picturesque Rose Cottages down by the river. She'd made the reservation thinking she'd be finished with Zach tonight. Instead, she'd asked for a late checkout, planning to get some sleep there tomorrow before she drove back to the ranch. There was no way she was spending even half the night at the Caspian Hotel, not with the memories of Lucky flitting at the edges of her brain.

Then finally, since she couldn't tell Travis she was spending a couple of days in Lyndon without making a point of visiting her brother Seth, she drove to the mayor's residence on Bainbridge Avenue, pulling the truck up to the historic, white, pillar-fronted three-story house. She truly missed the sleek, shiny Audi she'd leased over the course of the campaign.

Hopping out, she settled her sandals on the concrete driveway, smoothed her blouse, fluffed her hair and strode up the wide steps to the over-height double doors. It was nearly eight o'clock, so she knew she wouldn't disturb dinner.

It was Lisa Thompson who answered.

"Hey, Abigail," she greeted with a beaming smile. "Nice blouse. You look great!"

"Thanks." A warm feeling settled in Abigail's stomach. She liked being pretty. She really did.

"So, how're things at the ranch?" Lisa stepped to one side so that Abigail could enter the formal, octagonal foyer. The house had been built in 1902 and kept lovingly restored by the Lyndon Historical Society. The huge, overhead chandelier sparkled with light, while the marble floor gleamed, and notable, historical Lyndon City figures peered stoically down from gilt-framed oil paintings.

Male voices rose and fell from the depths of the house, something to do with land zoning and property tax. It didn't surprise Abigail in the least that her brother was conducting business into the evening.

"It's all good at the ranch," she answered Lisa's question.

"I didn't know you were coming to town." Lisa closed the door behind them, her black ballet flats whispering as she moved.

"Just picking up a few things," Abigail made the excuse.

"Spurs and saddle soap?" Lisa teased.

Apart from Zach, Abigail hadn't confessed to Lisa or anyone else her trepidation about going back to the ranch. She pasted on a smile. "A new pocketknife and some baling wire."

Lisa laughed. "Around you, I feel so useless."

"*You* are anything but useless. I don't know how my brother got by without you."

"I think he had a whole lot more fun before I showed up. Hey, Seth," Lisa called. "Your sister's here."

Conversation stopped in the back room. It had once been the original kitchen and dining area, but years ago it was converted into a large gathering room where many of the mayor's formal parties took place. A new kitchen had been added to the house sometime in the fifties and updated every decade since.

"Which one?" Seth called.

"It's me," Abigail called. "But you don't need to—"

Seth headed through the curved archway that led into the living room adjacent to the foyer. "Hey, Abby." He strode across the big room and pulled her into his usual hug. "What are you doing in town?"

"A little shopping," she told him cheerfully. "What's up with the zoning?"

He pulled back and waved a dismissive hand. "The usual. The chamber of commerce wants the town boundaries extended past the river bend, and the ranching community is up in arms over the grazing leases. You staying over?"

"I already checked into Rose Cottages."

He frowned. "Why would you do that? You know we've got plenty of room here."

"I plan on sleeping in tomorrow," Abigail lied.

"So what?"

"So, you're here. And you'll be up early. Not everybody wants to keep your manic schedule," she added.

"You've never minded my schedule. In fact, I think you liked it."

"Well, I'm not working for you anymore. And I feel like being self-indulgent."

"And so you should," Lisa stoically defended, linking an arm through Abigail's in blatant solidarity. "Give the girl a break. She'll be up slopping the hogs at the crack of dawn soon enough."

"We don't have hogs," said Seth. He turned, calling out, "Benjamin?"

"Yes?" a young man's voice answered from the gathering room.

"Do you mind running over to Rose Cottages and grabbing Abigail's suitcase?"

"Seth!" Abigail protested, reflexively moving to block the door. She was not going to let herself get shanghaied.

"I'm not letting my sister stay in a hotel."

"And I'm not letting my brother order me around."

Benjamin, a local teenager who was doing a part-time internship with Seth, appeared in the doorway. A bedraggled, black-and-white puppy limped in at his heels, sniffing its way around the legs of a colonial side table.

"Which cottage are you in?" Seth asked Abigail.

She jerked her attention back to her brother. "*None* of your business."

"Don't start, Abby," Seth warned.

"Back off," she responded. She was usually quite amiable when it came to her family's desires, but she couldn't give in this time.

"I just opened a bottle of ninety-six St. Germain," he cajoled.

"I'm not thirsty."

"Come on."

"Boss," Lisa put in, in a warning tone. "Didn't we talk about this?"

Abigail was a little surprised that Lisa was willing to come to her defense. Lisa was brash and bossy at the best of times, but she was usually quite deferential to Seth.

"This is an entirely different circumstance," he intoned.

"It's exactly the same circumstance."

"What?" Abigail couldn't help asking.

"Problem solved," said Lisa, propelling Abigail from the room. "She'll stay at Rose Cottages, but join us for a drink now. Bring some glasses, Seth." Then she lowered her voice, leaning toward Abigail's ear. "So, what's going on?"

"Nothing," Abigail whispered in reply.

"Like hell," Lisa harrumphed as they made their way toward the gathering room. "You've got something going on tonight, or you wouldn't be fighting with Seth over where you slept." Then she raised her voice as they switched rooms. "Luis, Harlan, you remember Seth's sister Abigail."

Both men came to their feet from a sofa grouping where they were going over some kind of report.

"Nice to see you again." Luis nodded.

"Hi, Abigail," Harlan echoed.

She barely had a chance to say hello because Lisa kept her moving toward an alcove with a bay window. Tucked into the corner of the L-shaped room, it was furnished with a low, round table, several broad-leaf plants and a half-round, floral-print bench seat.

"Are you okay?" Lisa asked with obvious concern as they plunked down on the soft cushions.

"I'm fine," Abigail assured her, putting on a smile.

Lisa's eyes narrowed. "Something's off."

"No, it's not," Abigail lied.

The quick denial seemed to pique Lisa's curiosity. "It's just us girls…"

"There's nothing going on."

"Really?"

"Yes."

Lisa tsk-tsked. "It's a good thing you don't have to lie for a living."

"I'm not lying. Why would I be lying?" Abigail glanced to where her brother had followed them into the room. She wondered if he'd take Lisa to task or pick up his argument with Abigail. But, instead, he paused to joke with Luis and Harlan while he poured the wine.

"Because you're embarrassed, or you're up to no good. Or, hey, here's one, you're going to see that guy again. Making it a two-night stand."

Abigail felt her face heat up. She couldn't think of a single thing to say.

The men's voices rumbled and glasses clinked. The puppy scampered its awkward way over the patterned carpet toward them.

Lisa's eyes went wide, and her mouth formed an O. "No way."

"Exactly," Abigail told her firmly. "No way."

"You *are* planning a two-night stand."

"I'm not. No. Definitely not."

"You do realize you're protesting way too much."

"I'm protesting exactly the right amount because you're dead wrong." Dead wrong. The very last thing in the world Abigail was about to do was sleep with Zach again.

"Ladies," Seth's voice preceded him. He strode forward, offering each of them a crystal goblet of merlot.

"Thanks," Abigail managed to say, scanning his expression to gauge if he'd overhead anything.

"You're a very good mayor," Lisa told him approvingly as she accepted the other glass of wine.

"You might want to remember that," Seth retorted.

"How could I forget? It's in every other speech. Now go away." She shooed him with the back of her hand. "We're having girl talk."

"Yes, ma'am." He backed off with good humor.

Lisa returned her attention to Abigail. "You've got me worried here. You're acting weird."

Abigail heaved a sigh. If she was acting weird, she couldn't help herself. She wasn't any good at this cloak-and-dagger stuff.

"Fine." She took a bracing drink of her wine. "I am meeting someone tonight. But it's not what you think."

Lisa leaned in. "A man someone?"

"Yes, a man. But it's not like that. I'm helping him—" She stopped herself, searching for the right words. "It's a research project."

"A *research project?* At night? What is this, freshman year?"

"It really is a research project."

"Uh-huh." Lisa slipped off her flats and curled one leg beneath her simple, sky-blue dress. She gave an exaggerated sigh. "I'm envious of your private life."

"You really ought to focus on your own," Abigail advised.

"It's not the same. There's nothing going on in mine."

"I don't believe you," Abigail challenged, seizing on the opportunity to change the topic from herself to Lisa.

But Lisa wasn't so easily swayed. "You're the one with the hot guys on speed dial."

"Nobody's on speed dial."

"Then how're you contacting him?"

"He's not a hot guy."

"You're blushing again."

"Okay, he is a hot guy." Abigail regretted admitting there was a guy involved. "But it's not about sex."

Lisa chuckled. "It's always about sex."

"Do tell." Abigail raised her brows meaningfully, trying again to switch the focus to Lisa.

"I wish," Lisa scoffed.

"There must be somebody. You've been in Lyndon for three months now."

"I've been busy. Working hard. As you well know."

"What about the guys on the campaign?" Abigail glanced at Luis and Harlan. She caught Seth looking at Lisa, a funny expression on his face.

Lisa's earlier challenging and teasing of Seth came rushing back.

"What about Seth?" she blurted out.

Lisa's jaw dropped, and her cheeks flamed.

"Ah-ha!" said Abigail. "I knew there was something—"

"Not Seth." Lisa adamantly shook her head.

"Hey, I know he's your boss, but—"

"Not *Seth*," Lisa repeated, the flush turning to pallor as her gaze flicked across the room.

Abigail reached out. "What is it?"

"Nothing."

"What's going on?"

Lisa mutely shook her head.

Abigail couldn't help another glance to her brother. His brow furrowed as he watched their exchange. She pasted a smile on her face and rose to her feet, reaching for Lisa's arm. "Let's step outside."

Obviously upset, Lisa complied, and the two moved through an open set of French doors to a wide veranda that overlooked the mansion's extensive gardens. The scent of roses permeated the air, and crickets chirped over the backdrop of the light traffic on the distant interstate.

They stopped beside the far railing.

"Dish," Abigail ordered.

Lisa pushed back her blond hair and squeezed her eyes shut.

"I won't give you up," Abigail promised in a quieter tone, knowing Lisa had to have fallen for Seth. "You're not the only one who can keep a secret."

Lisa blinked open her blue eyes. "You sure?"

"Positive."

Lisa downed her remaining wine. "Oh, man. I can't—" She closed her eyes for another long second. "Okay. Fine. It's better than you thinking I've got the hots for Seth."

"Okay…" Abigail waited, not exactly sure what would be so terrible about being attracted to Seth.

Lisa looked directly into Abigail's eyes. "You know about Nicole, right?"

"Who's Nicole?"

"Nicole Aldrich. Your mother's younger sister."

Abigail drew back in surprise. She hadn't heard that name in years. "I know she died young," Abigail allowed. "I never met her, of course. And nobody really talks about her."

"She died at eighteen, right after I was born."

Abigail stilled. Then a tingle rushed over her skin. Her heart expanded in her chest. Could Lisa be saying…? "And…?" Abigail prompted impatiently.

"And I'm definitely not attracted to Seth," Lisa stated with a toss of her head. "As it happens, I'm his cousin."

Abigail gave a muted squeal, every muscle in her body contracting in delight. "And *my* cousin. *Our* cousin." She wrapped Lisa in a tight hug. "Why on earth wouldn't you tell us?"

"I didn't know how you'd feel."

Abigail drew back. "I feel great. How could you not know we'd be thrilled?"

Lisa gave a self-conscious laugh. "Because I didn't know you. That first day, I was just going to check you out. And you all assumed I was a campaign volunteer, and it seemed easier to go along with that. And then I found out about your dad, and that your mom was away. And then Seth hired me, and I loved the job, and I started to get scared that if he knew…"

"You thought Seth might fire you for being our cousin?"

"I thought he might fire me for secretly spying on him."

Seth's dry voice interrupted. "He might fire you for lying to him."

Lisa jerked back, her attention shifting to where Seth had silently appeared on the deck. "I never lied."

"You never told the truth."

"I was working up to it."

Seth crossed his arms over his chest. "And you pumped me for information."

"I did," Lisa admitted. "Your mother wasn't around, and you were the only one old enough to remember Nicole."

"I was six when she ran away."

Abigail glanced from one to the other. "I don't understand. When she died, why didn't they bring you to us?"

"About a week before the car accident, she left me with the Sisters of Charity—anonymously."

"You were abandoned? Raised by nuns?" Abigail couldn't help asking, her brain scrambling about a hundred miles an hour as she cataloged the revelations.

Lisa shook her head. "I was adopted by a wonderful family. It was only two years ago when I started looking for you. Records were sketchy, so it took a while—"

"And you're positive it's us?" Seth challenged.

Abigail socked her brother in the arm. "This is *good* news, Seth."

"I'm not after your money," Lisa protested.

"But you were after a job."

"Go away, Seth," Abigail ordered tartly, grasping Lisa's hand. "If you can't play nice with our new cousin, you can go do something else."

"I'm not going away."

"I'm sorry," Lisa offered to Seth. "I was scared."

Seth's expression seemed to soften. But there was a moment of meaningful silence before he spoke. "I do get it." Then he sighed and his arms dropped back to his sides, while the corners of his mouth turned up. "I knew there was something I liked about you."

A tremulous smile grew on Lisa's face, and she blinked rapidly. "Yeah?"

"It must be the stellar genes."

"It must be."

Seth's hand went to his chin. "I'm not sure how I feel about Travis and me being outnumbered four to two."

Abigail laughed in relief. "I can't wait to tell my sisters Mandy and Katrina."

Just then, the puppy scampered out the open door, skidding on the deck as it clumsily rounded the corner.

"So, you're heading back to the ranch tomorrow?" Seth asked Abigail.

"Yes." Abigail's own complex life came back to her in a rush. She hoped it was true. She hoped she could map something out for Zach in one night, catch a nap at Rose Cottages then head home. If not, well, she'd have to make up a new excuse for tomorrow night.

"Good," said Seth, reaching down to scoop the gawky puppy up in one hand. "Take this guy with you, will you?" He rubbed his chin on the top of the puppy's head. "He's the last of the litter, and they were going to put him down. He has a gimpy leg, blind in one eye, and he's got one ear up and one ear down. Nobody wanted him."

"Uh…" Abigail didn't know how to refuse. What the heck was she going to do with the puppy between now and when she went back to the ranch?

But Seth dropped the puppy into her arms. "Butch and Zulu will make a man out of him."

"He is a bit skittish," Lisa put in as she reached out to pet the pup.

Abigail tried to protest. "I'm not sure I can—"

"We named him Ozzy," said Seth.

"Now, that's just mean." Abigail felt a sudden rush of protectiveness for the pathetic puppy.

"No, I like it," Lisa interjected. "It's not like we could name him Spike or Killer."

"I guess not," Abigail slowly agreed. She had to admit, Ozzy would probably be happy at the ranch. As long as he learned to stay away from the horses and the cattle, it was pretty much doggie heaven. And Butch and Zulu were good with smaller animals. They didn't even bother the cats.

But she wasn't going back there for at least twenty-four hours. "Can I pick him up tomorrow?"

Lisa gave her a curious look, and she could see the wheels turning inside her newly discovered cousin's head. The last thing Abigail wanted to do was reprise their conversation about her plans.

"Never mind," Abigail quickly said. "He can sleep in my cottage tonight."

She hoped Zach liked dogs. And she hoped Ozzy liked road trips. They had a ways to drive before she could settle him in his new home.

Five

The pathetic little puppy scampered across the hardwood floor of Zach's compact suite on the third floor of the castle. He side-swiped the sofa, canted out of control and bumped his head against the ottoman, giving a little yelp.

Abigail glanced up from where she was typing on Zach's laptop. He'd set her up at the small dining table in one corner of the living area and logged her onto the company network.

"He's blind in one eye," she explained.

"He's also a little lopsided," Zach noted, observing Ozzy's odd gait. One front leg was shorter than all the others. The puppy sniffed his way along the fireplace hearth.

"That's why nobody wanted him." Abigail paused in her typing and turned in her chair.

Zach let his gaze rest on her pretty face. She'd changed into a feminine blouse and a pair of snug-fitting black jeans that showed off her curves. Her shoes were sexy now, too. She'd told him she'd stopped by her brother the mayor's mansion in Lyndon. He supposed the mansion had a stricter dress code than Craig Mountain. Or maybe it was because she liked her brother enough to dress up for him—unlike the way she felt about Zach.

"Do you always take pity on strays?" he asked.

The puppy plunked himself down at Zach's feet, gazing hopefully up at him with big brown eyes. Since Zach's heart wasn't made of stone, he lifted Ozzy into his lap.

"One more out at the ranch won't make a difference."

"You could have said no."

She shrugged. "Why would I?"

Zach felt a sudden curiosity about this welcoming family utopia that was apparently the Jacobs ranch. He speculated how much of her description translated into real life.

She turned back to the laptop. "How many new jobs will the Craig Mountain expansion create?"

"I don't know yet."

"Got a guess?"

"Why?"

Ozzy settled into Zach's lap.

"There are three mandatory exemptions to the water-license moratorium. One, if a state of emergency is declared in the region. Two, if a strategic regional industry is threatened. Or, three, if the issuing of the license or variance has a fundamental impact on employment creation in the region."

"Maybe a dozen new jobs," he reasoned. "Give or take."

She frowned. "That doesn't sound like much of an impact."

"Can we argue that beer is strategic?"

"This *is* cowboy country." She allowed what seemed like a reluctant smile along with her answer.

"And who has to declare the state of emergency?"

"The governor."

"So, not me."

She ended up smiling at that one, too. "Not you."

"So much for a mandatory exemption."

She hit a few keys. "Our other option is to make representation to the committee."

Ozzy shifted his little body, whimpering in his sleep, and Zach smoothed his palm down the puppy's soft coat. "How do we do that?"

"We fill out form 731-800(e) and submit appendix Q along with supporting documentation and letters of intent."

"I should be paying you to do this."

She typed out a sentence on the screen. "You think money's going to make me feel any better about the situation?"

Ozzy shifted again and twitched, his eyes blinking open.

"It would make *me* feel better."

"You should feel great. You're getting exactly what you want. Free of charge."

Ozzy whined and twisted, sniffing at the arm of the chair.

"Any chance this little guy needs a walk?" asked Zach.

Abigail paused to look at them. She grimaced. "Probably, he does."

"Okay, champ," Zach rose, lifting Ozzy to the floor and brushing traces of black-and-white fur from his lap.

"Care to check out the grounds?" he asked Abigail. The walk would be a whole lot more fun if she came along.

"Sure," she agreed. She quickly rose and headed directly for the suite door, obviously considering time of the essence.

The three of them made their way down the narrow hall, along a back staircase to the second floor, where they picked up the grand staircase that led to the foyer.

The ancient hinges creaked as Zach pushed open one side of the heavy, oak doors. He couldn't help admiring Abigail as she passed by. There was a sinuous grace in her movements, and unconscious sensuality in the sway of her hips, the tilt of her chin and the silky flow of her hair.

"The mayor's office has a dress code?" he asked, falling in behind her as they crossed the lighted porch toward the illuminated front grounds. Stars were scattered in the black sky, while the moon rose above the northern horizon.

"I did a little shopping in town." There was a hint of censure in her tone. "Had some time to kill this afternoon."

"Sorry about that."

She shrugged as they started down the wide, stone steps. "Oh, well, I needed a manicure anyway."

He glanced down at her fingers, noting what must have been her favorite lavender color. "I guess ranch work can be hard on the hands."

Ozzy chugged enthusiastically ahead, beelining for a clump of shrubbery.

"A little," she allowed, following in the general direction of the puppy.

As she stepped onto the thick lawn, she stumbled in her high shoes. Zach quickly reached out to grab her, steadying her with a hand at her hip, another on her shoulder. His body's reaction was instantaneous. His muscles zipped tight, and his senses went on high alert. Her soft scent surrounded him, and he remembered her taste, craved the feel of her in his arms.

"I'm fine," she insisted, pulling to get away.

But his brain was slow to react. He didn't let go.

"I'm *fine,*" she repeated, jerking back.

He forced himself to release her.

He cleared his throat. "So, how are things going back home?"

"Fine." She made a show of straightening her blouse.

"You're really not much of a conversationalist, are you?" But he knew it wasn't true. He'd talked to her for hours on end that first night, one topic flowing into the other, discovering a shared sense of humor and shared opinions on books, films and many current news events.

"You know perfectly well how I feel about the ranch," she pointed out.

"I do," he allowed.

"So, why do you think I'd want to talk about it?"

"Exactly how unhappy are you?" Not that he could fix it for her. But he realized he would if he could.

She tossed her auburn hair and lifted her pert nose. "I'm not unhappy at all."

"I didn't take you for a liar."

"And I didn't take you for a blackmailer."

They faced each other, and the night air seemed to smolder between them. Every nuance of their lovemaking rushed back to him. He searched deeply into her eyes, subconsciously easing closer. His hands twitched with the need to reach out to her. But it wouldn't be right, and it wouldn't be fair. She'd made her position clear, and he'd already made the hard choice between his company and his feelings for her. There was nothing left but for him to be a gentleman.

"I really do like you, Abby," he allowed himself.

"Funny, I don't like you at all."

"Liar," he whispered.

"Not about that." But her golden eyes had gone liquid, cheeks flushed, and her lips softened in the glowing light. Her chest rose and fell with deep, indrawn breaths.

Zach threw propriety to the wind. "Tell me you don't want me to kiss you."

"I don't want you to kiss me."

He shook his head. "I guess that was predictable."

She pivoted sharply away from him, taking a couple of steps across the lawn. "Ozzy?" she called. "Where are you, puppy?"

Zach glanced around the expanse of lawn, searching for the pup's movement. The lawn was night black, interspersed with pools of lamplight. He squinted to find the flashes of white in Ozzy's mottled fur.

"Ozzy?" Abigail called again, voice louder this time.

They heard a yelp, then a whimper. It was from the direction of the cliffs.

Abigail glanced back. "Zach?"

"He probably banged into a boulder." But Zach quickened his steps, striding toward the rocky ledges that overlooked the lake.

Ozzy whimpered again, and the sound of the waves grew louder.

Abigail took a few running steps, catching up to Zach. He saw that she'd stripped off her shoes.

"Wait here," he instructed as they came to the edge of the lawn. "The rocks are sharp."

"Ozzy?" she called.

The puppy let out a long whine.

Zach zeroed in on the sound. "I'll get him," he assured Abigail.

Walking carefully from rock to rock, skirting the biggest boulders, he made his way toward the cliff edge. He'd been out here this afternoon, so he knew it was dangerous terrain. He also had a pretty good idea of how close he could safely get to the edge.

Ozzy barked, and Zach stopped, looking right.

In the traces of moonlight, he could just make out the shape of the puppy. He'd either jumped or fallen into a rocky depression that boxed him in. It couldn't have been more than two feet deep, but he seemed perplexed by the task of climbing back out.

Zach chuckled low, squatting on his haunches to reach down.

"You poor, poor thing," he muttered, scooping his palm under the pup's belly.

Ozzy went limp with compliance, content to have Zach lift him out. Zach secured him against his chest.

"Got him," he called out to Abigail, rising to make his way back across the uneven ground.

She looked relieved as they approached.

"He's a bit of a candy-ass," said Zach. "I hope ranch life won't be too tough for him."

She reached out and scratched the pup's head, her knuckles grazing Zach's chest, causing him to suck in a breath.

"Kind of reminds me of my sister Katrina."

"Katrina?"

"Yes, she's a gorgeous, graceful ballerina in New York. But ranch work was too much for her."

"So, she gets to live her dream instead?"

"She does." There was pride in Abigail's eyes as she glanced up. "She's a principal dancer with the Liberty Ballet in New York City."

"But you don't get to live yours?" he asked.

"She started boarding school when she was ten years old. She only comes back for visits, not to work the ranch."

"So?"

"So, it's a completely different thing."

"I don't see how."

"That's because you're not trying." She dropped her hand and headed for the castle.

He began walking next to her. "I'm simply pointing out a double standard."

"What've you got against my family, anyway?"

"I've never even met most of them."

"But you're judging them."

"I'm judging you. And your apparent unwillingness to stand up to them."

"I don't hate ranching, Lucky."

She didn't appear to notice her use of his nickname, and he wasn't inclined to correct her. He liked hearing that name on her lips.

"Life isn't about doing things you 'don't hate.' It's about doing things you love."

"Easy for you to say. I'm sure your family has absolutely no problem whatsoever with you being a rich, successful brewery owner."

"I don't have a family."

"I mean your parents. You already told me you don't have brothers and sisters."

"I don't have parents either."

She stopped to look at him. "Did they die?"

"They did. When I was two."

Her eyes widened. "Seriously."

Zach was long past the place where having been orphaned was a problem for him. It simply was. He nodded in answer to her question.

"Wow," her breath whooshed out.

"Happens to a lot of people," he told her.

"I know." She nodded. "So, were you adopted?"

"I grew up in foster homes. Well, foster homes when I was really little, then a group home."

"A group home?"

"Like an orphanage. But smaller and less, you know, Oliver Twist."

"Oh, Zach." She blinked a couple of times.

"It's fine." He gave her an encouraging grin. "This conversation isn't about me."

"It is now."

"No, it's not. I'm all grown up. Everything's good."

"But you have no family."

"I have Alex. And I have my company."

"But—"

"It's okay, Doll-Face. Now stop looking at me like that."

"I'm sad for you."

He rolled his eyes. "You should be sad about mucking out stalls, not about my misbegotten childhood."

"We have hands who muck out the stalls."

"That's good to hear." Zach turned to start back to the castle again, thinking Abigail's feet must be getting cold, and Ozzy was probably getting hungry.

They walked a few yards in silence, Ozzy snuggled contentedly against Zach's chest, watching the nighttime world go by.

"My cousin was adopted," said Abigail.

"That's nice."

"I only just met her tonight. I mean, well, I'd met her lots of times before. She was involved in Seth's campaign. But I only just found out tonight that she is my cousin."

"While you were down in Lyndon?"

"Uh-uh. We got to talking." Abigail paused. "We were talking about her and about Seth, and she blurted it out. She came here looking for us a couple of months back. We never even knew about her. Did you ever look for your family, Zach?"

"Nobody to look for."

"Did you ever think about trying?"

"The state of Texas had no wish to pay for my education and upbringing. Believe me, if there'd been long-lost relatives to foist me upon, they'd have found them."

Abigail fell silent at that. And they made their way to the castle and mounted the stairs, heading back inside. Though there'd been a few moments in Zach's childhood when he'd fantasized about finding some long-lost relatives, he was a realist. Even if there was somebody out there with a tenuous genetic connection to him, what would be the point in finding them? His life was what it was, and he fully intended to live it.

* * *

Abigail blinked open her eyes to bright sunlight. It took a couple of seconds to realize she was on Zach's couch. The laptop was on the coffee table in front of her, and she was covered in a soft quilt, a throw pillow tucked under her head.

She'd reviewed the annual reports from Zach's six breweries until her eyes blurred and her head began to pound. As near as she could remember, she must have dozed off around five. She wasn't sure how long she'd slept, but it wasn't nearly long enough. Her eyes were scratchy, and a painful pulse throbbed at the base of her neck.

The suite was completely quiet.

She pulled into a sitting position, checking her watch and discovering it was nearly 10:00 a.m. She threw back the quilt then staggered her way to the bathroom, washing her face and scrubbing toothpaste across her teeth with her finger. She combed her hair and did the best she could to straighten her clothes. The small window provided a view of the front grounds and the parking lot. Several dozen vehicles were parked, and a number of people wandered the area. They looked more like tourists than employees, but she knew there'd be employees working both in the castle and the brewery by now. There would definitely be people down there who might recognize her. She suddenly felt like a princess imprisoned in a tower.

Ozzy's little nails clattered on the living-area floor, and she opened the bathroom door.

"Morning," Zach intoned, setting a tray down on the small corner table.

"You let me sleep," she accused, slipping out of the bathroom.

"You were exhausted. I slept, too."

"I should have gone back to Lyndon."

Delicious aromas rose as Zach removed the silver covers from the tray. "You were way too tired to drive."

"But it's daytime and I'm not supposed to be here."

"Nobody'll see you up here."

"So, I'm your prisoner?"

He lifted a silver pot and began to pour coffee. "You do have a flare for the dramatic."

She was drawn to the coffee, and moved across the room. "Can I leave?"

"Not in the daylight."

"There you go. I'm not being dramatic, I'm simply stating the facts at hand."

He grinned in response to her indignation. "You need anything?"

"Coffee." She lifted one of the cups and took a grateful sip. "I don't do well on five hours' sleep."

"Cream or sugar?"

"Straight up is fine with me."

"Like a cowboy?" he joked.

"I can do it over a campfire if necessary."

"Not necessary this morning." He gestured to the fine china and silver. It was quite beautiful.

"Where'd you get this stuff?"

"I think it might be antique." He pulled out a chair and gestured for her to sit down. It seemed pointless to argue, so she sat.

"Lucas is lobbying to open a small restaurant here at the brewery," Zach continued, taking the chair across from her. "He says people like touring the castle as much as they like touring the brewery, and this would help make Craig Mountain a destination."

"Seems like a good idea to me." Abigail helped herself to a small pot of strawberry jam and spread it on a slice of toast.

"I'd only consider it if it helped to market the beer."

"You don't want to diversify?"

"We're not a bed-and-breakfast."

"Could've fooled me." She bit down on the toast.

Zach chuckled. "These are extraordinary circumstances."

Abigail contemplated while she chewed and swallowed. "Zach, how many people do you think you could reasonably employ in a new restaurant?"

He raised his brows. "Are you thinking about the employment exemption?"

"We're definitely not going to get anyone to declare a state of emergency. And we'll never sell you as a strategic industry."

"I can ask Lucas. But I'm guessing, maybe twenty."

She knew it wouldn't be enough. "Even combined with the additional brewery staff, I don't think that'll work. You'd need to be adding a couple hundred new jobs at least."

"That's definitely not going to happen," said Zach, cutting into the omelet on his plate.

"Then we're back to the committee presentation."

"What about job losses if we close?"

"Those don't count."

"Why not?"

She shrugged. "I guess because every business in the valley that wanted a change to their license would threaten to close."

"How long do you think the committee process will take?"

"Weeks, at least. The application will take a while to write, and there's no guessing how long the committee will take to review it." The process was going to be longer than she'd hoped, that was for sure.

Zach set down his fork. "The bulldozers show up tomorrow."

"What bulldozers?"

"First thing we need to do here is dig the foundation for the expansion."

She sat up straight. "You're starting already?"

"I've got no choice. If we're not up and running by November, and into increased production by January, we won't make our spring orders."

"But—"

"There's no point in me sitting on my hands while you fill out the paperwork."

"But what if you don't get the license?"

He lifted his coffee cup in a mock salute. "I'm counting on you, Abigail."

Her stomach instantly hollowed out. He'd already told her DFB was in financial trouble. He was about to spend hundreds of thousands, if not millions, of dollars on what might be useless renovations.

"*Don't* count on me," she begged. Then she reflexively reached for his hand. "Seriously, Zach. This a long shot." She could fill out the paperwork for him, but many had tried this route. So far nobody had been successful.

His steel gaze moved from her hand to her face. "I don't have a choice."

She squeezed. "Of course you have a choice. You can wait to spend your money until we know for sure whether you're getting the variance."

"The clock's ticking."

"This is a mistake."

"It's a risk, not a mistake."

She swallowed, letting go of his hand and pushing back from her breakfast. Then she closed her eyes for a long second, knowing she had to be honest with him. "You're not going to get it, Zach. They're not going to grant you license variation."

"They will if you help me."

She shook her head. "I'm not magic. I'm trying because you're forcing me to try, but it's not going to work."

"We don't know that yet."

She rose to her feet, pacing to the window. "Lucky, you're living in denial. Don't do it. Call off the bulldozers. It's too big a risk."

He rose more slowly. "Everything I've ever done in life has been a risk."

"Not like this."

"Exactly like this. If I wait any longer, there'll be no point in even getting the license, because we'll lose the spring orders and the company will go under."

She advanced on him. "The Craig Mountain expansion will tie a brick to the entire company and drag it straight down to the bottom."

His dark eyes seemed to pin her in place. "You can do this, Abby."

She slowly shook her head.

He placed a reassuring hand on her shoulder. "I know you can."

"Don't put this on me. It's too much. I can't be responsible—"

"I'm only asking you to do your best."

For some reason, her eyes stung. "My best won't be good enough."

He stepped forward, gathering her in his arms and holding her in a comforting embrace. He spoke against the top of her head. "It'll be good enough."

Her voice was muffled against his chest. The thought of having that much riding on her work was overwhelming. "Let me quit. Let me go home."

"I can't do that."

He continued to hold her, and the warmth of his body seeped into hers. She breathed in his scent and fisted her hands against the overwhelming rush of desire that swarmed her. She wanted to hug him back, to hold him close, to kiss him hard and deep and bury her emotions in the passion she knew they'd find all over again.

He drew back, gazing down at her, palms rubbing circles against her shoulders.

She told herself to step away. She had about five seconds to make the right choice. His eyes darkened, and his lips parted. She knew that expression, could feel the pulse of his thoughts. She held her breath as he bent forward.

She forced herself to jerk back. "No."

The word stopped him cold. His jaw clenched, and his hands convulsed, squeezing her shoulders for a second longer.

"We can't," she managed to say.

He dropped his hands and stepped back, voice clipped. "Sorry."

She turned her head, afraid to look at him while she gave a short nod. "I'll get back to work."

"Yeah."

She heard him turn. Heard the clatter of Ozzy's footsteps. Heard the door open then close, and their sounds disappeared.

* * *

Zach slouched in a dusty, French-provincial chair in the topmost reaches of a castle tower, Ozzy curled sleeping in his lap, and his cell phone squeezed in one hand as the bulldozers rumbled into the rear, gravel parking lot. Alex was speed-dial one, but Zach couldn't bring himself to press the button just yet.

Abigail had agreed to stay another day. She'd made it crystal clear that she had her doubts about their success with the license. Truth was, he had his doubts, too. But he couldn't dwell on that. There was only one route forward.

He'd signed off on the construction contract this morning, and it was the right thing to do. It was the only thing to do. In his experience, any action was better than no action. He knew that if he sat here and did nothing, the company would trickle down to an inevitable death.

He pressed his thumb on the one key and lifted the phone to his ear.

Alex picked up on the first ring. "Hey, Zach."

The clatter of background noise quickly faded as Alex obviously moved to a different location.

"How's it going?" Zach asked his business partner.

"I just found out that Shetland Trucking went bankrupt," Alex rattled off in a matter-of-fact voice. "There's a mechanical breakdown at the bottling plant in Charlotte. And Stephanie walked out on me last night. So, pretty much business as usual."

"Again?" Zach asked.

"Which part?"

"Stephanie."

"It was inevitable," said Alex.

"She serious this time?"

"If she's not, I am. I don't know what other guys do, but I'm not into working sixteen-hour days then coming home to talk about my feelings."

"So, how're you feeling about that?" Zach couldn't help joking.

"Shut up."

"We can talk about it if you like."

"Then can we braid each other's hair?"

"You get a new trucking company?" Zach went back to business.

"As of this morning. What about you?"

"I'm looking at the bulldozers now."

"Fantastic. So, you got the license?"

"Not yet."

Alex paused. "What do you mean, not yet?"

"Abigail's still working on it."

Another pause. "But you started anyway?"

"We're out of time."

It took a minute for Alex to speak. "You're putting it all on one roll of the dice?"

"I am."

"And if we don't get the license?"

"Is that a rhetorical question?"

"It's a veiled criticism."

"You'd have done the same thing."

"Maybe. Probably." Alex heaved a sigh. "Hell, what've we got to lose?"

"Beer."

Alex coughed out a laugh. "At least we're both still employable as bartenders," he said, referring to the first jobs they'd had after they left the group home.

"I could start all over." Zach wasn't worried about himself. He'd give up the Houston penthouse, the sports car and his platinum credit card in the blink of an eye. Some of the happiest times of his life were when he and Alex had shared a tiny basement suite while they saved up the down payment for their first brewery.

But he'd hate to be forced to lay off even one employee. Many of them had kids and mortgages, and for the first time were settling into normal lives.

"Need a roommate while you start over?" asked Alex. "The apartment lease is in Stephanie's name."

"You're homeless?"

"I am."

"You've got my spare key."

"I guess it's either your place or the Four Seasons."

"Hey, we're on a budget now." Zach glanced at the third bulldozer rumbling and clanking its way off the trailer. If this all went bad, their days at the Four Seasons were definitely over.

"The Family Inn on Hawthorn Street?" Alex suggested.

"Get your ass to my place."

"Yeah, I probably will. How long do you think you'll be in Colorado?"

"A couple more days, anyway. Hopefully, Lucas can take it from there."

The aging door to the tower room creaked. Both Zach and Ozzy looked toward the sound. Abigail peeked around the end of the thick, oak panels.

"Gotta go," said Zach, meeting her eyes.

"Keep me posted."

"Will do."

"You'd better bring this one home," Alex warned.

It was probably the hundredth time Alex had said that to Zach over the years. They'd been in many tight spots before, taken plenty of risks, but this was truly a make-or-break moment.

"I know." Zach clicked off the phone and tucked it into the breast pocket of his shirt. "Hey."

"Hi." She moved around the end of the door and into the room, glancing at the curved walls, dusty furniture, boxes and crates, and the collection of knickknacks and outright junk that covered every horizontal surface.

"Wow," she breathed.

"Quite the collection," he acknowledged, dislodging Ozzy as he came to his feet.

"Don't get up."

"I'm already up."

She gave him a rueful grimace. "I just came to tell you that something's come up."

He didn't like the sound of that. "To do with the license?"

"To do with me. I have to go to Houston."

"Why?" Was it an excuse to get away from him?

"It's a long story. My parents are down there. And, well, I told you about Lisa, the newly discovered cousin? We need to tell my mom about her before other people find out. I just talked to Seth and then to Travis. They want me to do it. In person. Of all the sisters, I know Lisa best. And Katrina and Mandy are—"

"Living their own lives?"

"That's none of your business."

"I suppose not," he allowed. Though it still galled him that she seemed to be the one in the family bearing the most burden.

"I know you're in a hurry." Despite everything, there was an apology in her voice.

"We can keep working while you're in Houston," he pointed out. "In fact, it'll be easier. DFB headquarters is there."

"Whoa." She held up her palms. "I'm not going to have spare time in Houston."

"You won't be busy twenty-four seven."

"Zach—"

"Abby—"

"Abigail."

"Yeah, 'cause that's our biggest problem." It might not be fair to her, but he was frustrated by the situation. And he was getting genuinely worried about losing his entire company.

Her tone was tart. "I have to focus on my family right now. I'm sorry if it slows down your personal agenda for me, but I have obligations."

He pointed out the window. "See that? Do you have any idea how much it costs per hour to dig that hole?"

She tightened her jaw. "You don't own me, Zach."

"Maybe not, but we have a deal."

"I'm altering the terms."

"That's not your choice to make."

"Are you drawing a line in the sand?"

He was. But maybe that wasn't the smart choice. Maybe he'd pushed her as far as he could. It was time to change tactics. "You can have time with your family in Houston."

"Thank you so *very* much."

"But you'll also need to find time for me. Five other breweries are waiting to press the go button on spring orders. If I can't confirm Craig Mountain, I'm going to have a way bigger problem than a useless hole in the ground."

She hesitated, and her teeth came down on her bottom lip.

"I'll spring for your plane ticket." He sweetened the pot. "Hell, for your hotel, your meals, anything you need." He didn't give a damn about the cost.

"My sister Mandy's fiancé has a jet."

"He coming with us?"

"There is no us."

"I need you, Abby."

He realized the words were true on far too many levels.

"We can bring Ozzy," he offered. "He can stay in my penthouse."

She cracked a smile at that. "You're bribing me with a dog?"

"I am."

"You're going to spoil him," she accused. "And then he's going to hate me when I make him live at the ranch."

Zach bent and picked up the pup, scratching under his chin. "He really doesn't strike me as the ranch-dog type."

There was total sympathy in her eyes when she gazed at Ozzy.

"Fine." She capitulated. "You take the dog, and I'll see you in Houston. But I'm not promising anything. I'm going to be busy."

"Thank you," Zach offered sincerely.

"Are you ever going to be out of my life?"

He hesitated over his answer. What an intriguing question. He didn't really want to be out of her life. And he sure didn't want her out of his. Not yet, anyway, and it had nothing whatsoever to do with any water license.

Six

Abigail was happy to see her father looking so well. He'd been in rehab in Houston for several months following a stroke in the early summer. Luckily, her sister Mandy's fiancé had been in the valley with his jet plane that night, and they were able to whisk everyone to Lyndon and then Denver for his treatment. Ultimately, they moved him to a state-of-the-art facility in Houston. After months of therapy, he was nearly ready to come home to walk Mandy and Katrina down the aisle at their double wedding, coming up in a few weeks.

Now Abigail and her mother, Maureen, moved to a shady table in the lush garden of a restaurant a few miles from the facility. The scents of roses, asters and sage mingled beneath the oak trees in the September afternoon. They ordered iced tea and spinach, raspberry salads, settling comfortably into padded rattan chairs.

"And how's Travis doing with the ranch?" asked Maureen, stirring some sugar into her glass.

"He seems good," Abigail answered. "Though I've actually seen more of Seth lately than Travis."

"But you are back on the ranch."

"I was for a few days. But I'm back in Lyndon." Abigail drew a breath. "Speaking of which, your sister Nicole's name came up the other day."

A look of obvious shock contorted her mother's face. "Nicole?"

"You never talk much about her."

Her mother's fingers trembled ever so slightly as she rested them on the table. "Even after all these years, it's hard for me to think about her. She was so young and beautiful and full of life. It hurt a lot to lose her."

"Seth said she ran away from home?"

"Sadly, she did. All she could talk about back then was the bright lights and the big city. I tried to convince her to pick out a college." Maureen squared her slim shoulders. "But I couldn't. She thought she was going to become a model or an actress or some such craziness. Seven months later, she was in that accident."

"Seven months?" Abigail's stomach flip-flopped.

Maureen's eyes shimmered. "I can only guess what happened. I adored her. But she always partied too much, was constantly finding excuses to stay in town on weekends. She smoked and drank with her friends. There was no holding her back."

While her mother spoke, Abigail's brain did the math. The nuns had told Lisa she was two weeks old when her mother dropped her anonymously into their care. Nicole had died a week later. That made her ten or twelve weeks pregnant when she left town.

Lisa's father was from Lyndon. But that would have to wait until later.

"We were told the pair of them were leaving a bar," Maureen continued, a faraway look on her face. "We later found out his family didn't know Nicole, had never met her. They were estranged from their son, too." Maureen absently restirred the iced tea.

"Mom." Abigail reached forward and took her mother's hand.

"Yes, dear?"

"I have something to tell you. It's surprising, maybe even shocking."

Maureen frowned. "Are you ill, honey? Is something wrong?"

Abigail quickly shook her head. "No, no. Nothing like that. It's good news. At least I think it's good news."

Her mother waited.

"It's Nicole, Mom. She had a daughter."

Maureen blinked, her expression frozen in the dappled sunlight.

"A daughter," Abigail repeated. "She was adopted out to a very nice family. She started looking for us a couple of years ago. And now she's found us."

Maureen's voice was paper dry. "Nicole had a baby?"

Abigail smiled, squeezing her mother's hand. "My cousin. Your niece."

Maureen's eyes welled up with tears, and her hand went to her chest.

"Her name's Lisa," said Abigail, speaking more quickly. "I've met her. In fact, I know her. She helped with Seth's campaign."

"I can't believe it," said Maureen, but a smile was forming on her face. "Okay. I do believe it." The smile turned into a shaky laugh. "Nicole was never a careful or cautious person."

"So, you're okay? You'll like her. She's a wonderful woman."

"You said she helped on Seth's campaign? Is she in Lyndon?"

"She came to town a few months ago. But right now..." Abigail paused. "Right now, she's in Houston."

"She's here?"

"She wants to meet you. And she wants to meet Mandy and Katrina and everyone. But we wanted to start with you."

"Oh, well in that case." Maureen promptly stood up, dropping her napkin onto the table. "Let's go."

Abigail laughed. "Hold on."

Her mother paused, waiting.

"We don't have to go anywhere." Abigail nodded across the garden to a far table. "She's over there."

As Maureen turned to stare, Lisa caught the gist of the body language and came gracefully to her feet. She was wearing a white, sleeveless tank dress, her blond hair loose and framing her face. She looked nervous but brave as she walked forward on delicate, white, strapless sandals.

Abigail rose and moved to stand next to her mother as Maureen approached them.

"Nicole," Maureen whispered, groping blindly to grasp Abigail's hand. "She looks just like Nicole."

Abigail found her own eyes filling with tears.

Maureen let go of her hand, rushing forward to pull Lisa into her arms.

Lisa's eyes fluttered closed as Maureen rocked her back and forth and stroked her hair.

"Oh, my darling." Maureen spoke in a choked voice. "I'm so glad you've come home."

It didn't take Abigail long to realize Zach's employees were like a family. Thirty people worked in the executive offices, with another hundred and fifty or so between the sales, marketing, accounting and human resources offices on various floors in the office tower in downtown Houston. All of them greeted Zach by his first name. They all seemed to know he'd been in Colorado, and they were all anxious to hear how things were going with Craig Mountain.

She'd been in Houston for three days, and between visiting her father and watching her mother and Lisa get to know each other, she'd managed to power through the application for Zach. Now she sat in a corner boardroom on the thirty-second floor, gazing out the bank of windows at the lights of the surrounding buildings and the clear, night sky. The water-license variance application form 731-800(e) was on the table in front of her, neatly printed out, supported by charts and graphs, and a letter of intent, complete with the company background, prospectus and all the technical data she'd been able to pull together from her previous water-table research. It was a great report, probably the best she'd ever done.

Half the double doors opened, and Zach entered with his partner, Alex Cable. She'd met Alex earlier and really liked him.

He seemed smart and motivated, with a wry sense of humor. She knew he'd just broken up with his girlfriend. She also knew he was staying with Zach. Though Alex was fairer than Zach, with blue eyes, light brown hair and a lankier build, the two had a lot of gestures, expressions and speech patterns in common. If she hadn't known better, she would have taken them for brothers.

Zach glanced at the cover page of the report, then looked to Abigail. "That it?"

"That's it," she confirmed. She was done, officially free from his blackmail, ready to go back to her old life.

"It's really nice of you to help us out," Alex put in.

Abigail shrugged. "It was no problem." Then she caught Zach's ironic brow lift, and she amended the statement. "Uh, not much of a problem. I am glad to be finished, though."

Zach lifted the report and thumbed through it.

"We should celebrate," said Alex.

"You don't have a variance yet," Abigail pointed out, taking her clutch purse from the table and tucking it under her arm. She should be rushing from the room, but, for some reason, she found herself hesitating.

Her mother was resting at her rented condo right now, tired from her emotional few days with Lisa. She'd taken a shine to Ozzy, and the puppy was keeping her company. It was nearly eight o'clock, and Lisa had asked Abigail to meet for a late dinner or maybe hit a club before they flew back to Colorado in the morning.

It was a strange feeling of déjà vu. Abigail was having a final night on the town before heading back to the ranch. She was trying hard not to rehash the Lucky and Doll-Face evening in her mind, but it was proving impossible. She was also trying hard not to think about leaving Zach forever, but that was causing her trouble, as well. Despite everything that had happened, she couldn't seem to stop herself from liking him.

"How long will the committee deliberations take?" Zach asked.

"Weeks, probably," she answered, avoiding looking into his

eyes. She had to be strong for another five minutes or so, get out of here and forget about looking back.

"We don't have weeks."

"You don't have a choice."

"Anything we can do to speed it up?" asked Alex.

"You want to try bribing a legislative committee of the state of Colorado?"

Alex coughed out a laugh. "Not a good idea?"

"Not if you enjoy life outside the Colorado penal system," she responded. Then she shot a stern look at Zach. "And there's not a thing in the world you can blackmail me with on that one."

"Blackmail?" Alex glanced from one to the other, clearly in the dark about the details of her and Zach's working relationship. No matter. It was over now, and Zach could explain himself however he wanted.

"Ask your partner," she told Alex, starting for the door. "By rights, he should already be in jail."

"Who'd you blackmail?" asked Alex.

"She's exaggerating," Zach drawled.

"Abigail." Alex's voice stopped her.

She turned, prepared to answer his question, acknowledging that she'd been the one to drop this bomb into the conversation.

"He actually blackmailed you into helping us?"

It was all a moot point now, and she didn't really care enough to keep the secret from Alex. Mostly, she just felt tired. "He did."

"Go, Zach." Alex whistled in obvious admiration. "What'd he use?"

"He slept with me then threatened to tell my brothers."

"Abby." Zach dropped the report back onto the table.

"What?" She stared at him. "You embarrassed about sleeping with me, or embarrassed about committing a felony?"

"It wasn't like that," he protested.

"It was exactly like that. And now you've got what you want."

"I threatened to tell them you hated the ranch."

"I don't hate the ranch." Though she once again felt as if a set of walls was closing in on her. By this time tomorrow, she'd be in blue jeans and boots.

He moved toward her. "I was never going to kiss and tell."

She was vaguely aware of Alex discreetly backing his way out of the room.

"Then you lied to me," she told Zach as he came to a halt directly in front of her.

"I guess I did." His eyes reflected the desire she couldn't deny.

"Yet another sin on your head." But her pulse sped up at his proximity, and her skin flushed with heat.

"Yet another sin," he agreed. "You want to go get something to eat?"

She sputtered a laugh. "A date? On my last night in town?"

"Something like that."

"You looking for another one-night stand?"

He gently took her hand in his, rubbing the pad of his thumb over her knuckles. "Absolutely."

Her mounting desire peaked and crested. She struggled not to stammer. "You have got to be kidding."

He leaned in, voice lowering to a husky drawl. "I'll understand if you say no."

Her breath hitched. "How very magnanimous of you."

"But I'm still going to ask."

"I'm saying no," she managed to say.

"Yeah. I figured." But his hand moved up to her cheek. His fingers brushed her sensitized skin, and he dipped his head toward her. "At least let me kiss you goodbye."

She ordered herself to move, to back away, get out of the danger zone. But her feet weren't cooperating, and her head was tilting to accommodate him. Her lips were parting, and her eyes were fluttering closed.

When his lips touched hers, desire exploded within her. A small sound escaped from her throat. Her knees went weak, and her chest became a tight band of emotion. Before she could form a coherent thought, her arms wound their own way around his neck.

His free arm pulled her close, pressing their bodies together, while his tongue found its way into the hot recesses of her mouth. The kiss continued for long minutes before he broke it off.

"I've missed you," he moaned, cradling the back of her head, pressing her cheek against his strong chest.

Her voice was muffled. "You've barely let me out of your sight."

"You know what I mean."

She did. She'd missed him, too. But that didn't make sleeping with him again a good idea. Okay, it would be great. It would be fantastic. But it would also be foolish.

She shook her head and tried to pull back.

"I can't let you go."

"You have to." She swallowed, forcing herself to stay strong. "You're out of ammunition, and I'm going home."

She braced her hands on his shoulders and broke free of his arms, stumbling a couple of steps in her high heels.

He reached for her, but she'd already put enough space between them.

"Goodbye, Zach."

He stilled. But then he dropped his shoulders and gave a sad smile. "Goodbye, Doll-Face."

Her eyes started to burn, and she quickly turned away, walking out the door.

Watching her two sisters dancing under the sparkling lights of the central ballroom at the Ten Peaks Country Club in downtown Denver, Abigail couldn't stop smiling. Mandy's gown was clean and classic, strapless with simple lines that flowed gracefully as she danced in Caleb's arms. Katrina's dress had a sweetheart neckline and glittered with shimmering embroidery, beadwork and sequins. Where Mandy had gone with a silver-link necklace and hoop earrings, Katrina wore cascades of white sapphires, interlaced to a point just above her cleavage. Her dangling earrings and elegant bracelet made up the set. She looked delicate and beautiful in Reed's arms.

Abigail had served as maid of honor, while Lisa was a bridesmaid. Seth and Travis stood up for the grooms. Their father was sitting now, at the head table near the multitiered cake that was flanked by two bridal bouquets. But he'd done an impressive job of escorting his daughters down the aisle. After the wedding, he and Abigail's mother were definitely considering an extended stay here.

The lights were dim around the dance floor as everyone watched the two bridal couples in their first waltz. Abigail's feet were sore, but in a good way. It had been weeks since she'd worn high heels, and she felt feminine and beautiful in her knee-length, plum-colored bridesmaid dress. Made of airy chiffon, it had a soft, strapless bodice, a two-layer skirt and a sleek waistline.

"Abby?" A deep voice resonated close to her ear, sending a shiver down her spine.

She twisted to come face-to-face with Zach. She blinked, unable to make sense of his appearance.

"Hi," he offered.

"What are you *doing* here?"

He was dressed in a well-cut three-piece steel-gray business suit, his silver tie in a sharp knot, his crisp, white shirt allowing him to blend with the other guests.

"I need to talk to you," he whispered.

"I'm a little busy."

The crowd broke into applause as the final strains of the waltz came to a close. The string quartet immediately launched into another song.

Mandy picked Seth from the crowd, while Katrina laughingly asked Travis to dance. Reed Terrell snagged Abigail's hand and smoothly pulled her onto the hardwood floor. He swung her gracefully into his arms. For a large man, he'd always been a great dancer. He'd been a year ahead of her in high school, and they'd danced together many times before.

"Who's that?" he asked, leaning to be heard above the music.

Abigail glanced back at Zach. Her heart tripped at his handsome, sexy looks.

"Zach Rainer," she told Reed. "He owns Craig Mountain Brewery."

"He was invited to the wedding?" Reed's tone was incredulous.

"He's here looking for me."

Reed stopped.

"Don't," Abigail warned. She knew her neighbor well enough to realize he would step in to solve whatever problem was at hand. Dressed in a wedding tux or not, he was completely capable of tossing Zach out on his ear. "I'll handle it."

Reed hesitated a second longer, but to her relief began dancing again. "Why's he crashing my wedding?" he asked.

"I don't know yet. I haven't had a chance to talk to him."

"He a friend?"

"Sort of."

Reed stared down at her, eyes narrowed. "There something you're not telling me?"

She gave a light laugh. "There are many, many things I'm not telling you, Reed. But don't worry about it. It's all good."

"Are you in some kind of trouble?"

"Not at all." Unless you counted her overwhelming desire to haul Zach off to the nearest hotel room and ravage him. That was a whole lot of trouble.

"He looks ticked off."

"He's impatient."

"Well, he can bloody well wait until my wedding's over."

"Stop," Abigail ordered. "Katrina's going to kill me if I get you all riled up."

"I'm not riled."

"Yes, you are."

"You don't know riled, Abby."

Abigail grinned. "Welcome to the family." She stretched up and gave him a kiss on the cheek.

"You've got a great family," said Reed.

"It just got greater." She glanced at Caleb who was laughing with Lisa. "Two new brothers, and a new cousin."

"Seth just thanked me and Caleb for evening things up between the genders again."

"We women did have the upper hand there for a few weeks." The song wound down.

"You better get back to Katrina."

Reed scowled in Zach's direction one more time. "You let me know if he gives you any trouble."

"Absolutely," Abigail lied.

As Reed walked away, she felt someone come up behind her.

"Care to dance?" asked Zach.

She turned. "You're not supposed to be here."

"Like I told you, I need to talk to you."

"Can it not wait?"

Without waiting for permission, he drew her into his arms.

It seemed simpler to dance than to make a scene by arguing about it. Plus, that would bring Reed to her side in a heartbeat, so she went along with Zach.

He settled her close. "You want to meet up later instead?"

"I do not."

"It was worth a try."

"You crash my sisters' wedding, and now you're hitting on me?"

"I can't seem to help myself."

"Try, Zach. Try."

His tone stayed intimate, and his hand moved up and down her back, tracing the bare skin between her shoulder blades. "You take my breath away, Doll-Face."

She steeled herself against the softer feelings creeping into her psyche. "You see that guy over there? The groom? The one I was just dancing with?"

"I do."

"See how big he is? Well, he likes me. And he's already ticked off at you."

"I like you, too."

"You like me naked." The second the words were out of her mouth, Abigail realized they were a colossal mistake.

She mentally braced for his retort, but Zach didn't reply. Instead, he gathered her closer, seeming to mold his body to hers. She fought the arousal that gripped her body, but it was useless. Images of their night together were back in force.

"I need to talk to you," he repeated, voice barely a rasp. "And I can't wait. Can we go outside?"

His tone brought a thousand questions into her mind. Why was he here, after all these weeks? Had he missed her? Had he come back for her, to pursue their relationship?

She tried to control the hope that surged inside her. She realized in a split second that she wanted him to pursue her. She wanted to be with him again, free from all the complications that had tangled them in knots.

She gave him a mute nod, and he took her hand in his, leading the way from the dance floor to patio doors that led to a lighted garden. Conflicting thoughts continued to spin around in her mind. Sure, he lived in Houston, while she lived in Lyndon. But there were airplanes. There were hotels. Maybe they could spend weekends together someplace in the middle.

Anticipation tightened her chest as she realized she was going to say yes. If he wanted to try something long-distance, she'd agree to it. And then maybe they could find that nearest hotel right now and spend the night in each other's arms. Her breath caught and her heartbeat thudded deep.

He came to a halt at the far edge of the concrete patio, turning to face her, taking his hand from hers. The music and voices wafted out from the reception, while pot lights glowed softly from the hedges and garden beds, reflecting off the planes and angles of his face. He was an incredibly attractive man.

"Abby," he started.

"Yes?" She waited, not moving, not breathing.

"The application was rejected."

She blinked. It took a second for her brain to switch gears.

"The committee turned us down," he elaborated.

"The water license?" she all but stammered.

"Yes."

She took a shaky step back, mind refusing to accept reality. "You dragged me away from my sisters' wedding to tell me you didn't get your precious water license?"

He looked confused. "What else?"

Excellent question. She pressed her fingertips against one

temple. "Oh, I don't know. Nothing, I guess. What *is* your problem?"

"I just told you my problem."

"And this couldn't have waited until tomorrow?"

"You're leaving tomorrow."

"Yes, I am. Goodbye, Zach." She took a step toward the reception.

He snagged her upper arm. "Hear me out, Abby."

"No." She was not going to let him do this. She'd done her best. She'd caved to every single thing he'd asked of her. And to add insult to injury, she'd apparently become infatuated with him along the way.

"I need you."

She glared at him. "You need a bankruptcy attorney."

"You're giving up? Just like that."

"Just like that? There is no 'just like that.' I did everything I could, everything I could think of. Every fact, figure, argument and rationale I could dream up went into that paper, Zach. There is nothing, nothing more I have to offer."

"I don't believe you."

"Too bad."

He dropped his hand from her arm, raking it through his short hair. "There *has* to be something."

"There's nothing. You and a hundred companies like you want variances. The State has decided you can't have them right now. They've made a rule, and they're following it, Zach. You're just ticked because they won't break it for you."

"I'm not asking anyone to break the rules. I'm only asking for a little logic and reason."

"You're asking a government for logic and reason."

His lips flattened in obvious anger.

"You see the flaw in that, right?" she pressed.

"I see you giving up."

"This is not my problem."

"You're right. It's my problem. But while you stand there secure in that knowledge, Abby, ask yourself one thing." He stepped forward, crowding her. "Ask yourself what you would do if this was your family."

His gaze held hers, and she felt her resolve falter.

"If it was your ranch on the line. If it was Seth's and Mandy's and Katrina's and Travis's jobs. Would you throw up your hands in defeat? Or if you thought I could help, would you not track me down, back me into a corner and force me to agree?"

"By blackmailing you?" She'd like to think she wouldn't, but maybe she would.

"By any means possible."

Her throat became dry, and her voice became strained. "I tried to help you, Zach. I truly, truly tried."

He took the last step that brought him directly in front of her. "One more time?" he asked. "Tonight. When you're done here, before you go back to Lyndon. Let's think it through one more time. You and me."

There was no point. "I read every single word of the moratorium. I've looked up precedents and past cases. I followed their template to the letter. I dotted every *i,* I crossed every single *t.*"

"We're talking hundreds of jobs. Hundreds of people without anything but the livelihood and the family they get from working at DFB. A couple of hours, Abby. Can you give me that?"

Her mind screamed no. But there was something in the raw honesty of his plea that got to her.

"If it was your family?" he asked more softly this time, "what would you do?"

She tipped her chin and tossed her head, telling herself she was capitulating for a good cause. "Fine. We'll try one more time."

He was silent for a moment, almost as if he couldn't believe she'd finally said yes. "Thank you," he breathed, in obvious relief and gratitude.

She was hit with an unexpected rush of pleasure. Which was silly. She might feel good about helping him, but that didn't change the cold hard facts. "I wish I could be magic, Zach. I truly do."

He gently took her hands. "You are."

Despite everything, she wanted to throw herself into his arms, squeeze him tight and forget the rest of the world existed. "Go away," she murmured. "Leave me alone for the next few hours."

He nodded, and with a final, reflexive squeeze of his fingers, he let go and walked away.

She stared into the dark reaches of the garden, struggling to bring her emotions under control.

Lisa's voice came from behind her, skirt rustling, heels clicking rhythmically on the concrete as she approached. "Now, who the heck was that?"

Abigail shook her head and gave a helpless laugh. "Nobody."

"Come on. Anybody who looks at you that way is not a nobody."

Abigail was tired of keeping all this locked tight inside her chest. She gave in to temptation. "Cone of silence?"

"Cone of silence."

"That was my one-night stand."

Lisa whistled low, turning to look at the doorway where Zach had disappeared. "Oh, mama."

"You got that right." Abigail gave a wry grimace. "He was also my midnight research project. And tonight I'm meeting him after the reception."

"Really?"

"Yes."

"You okay?"

"No."

"You want to tell me what's going on?"

"Yes," Abigail admitted. "But I can't."

Lisa moved closer. "Oh, but you can."

"I really can't." Abigail hadn't gone to all this trouble to blurt the truth out to Lisa.

"I'm family now," said Lisa. "Plus, I'm discreet. And I'm not above feeding you champagne until you reveal every single secret locked away in your little heart." She nodded to a waiter standing just inside the doors. "You might as well do it without the hangover."

It was tempting.

Lisa rapidly rubbed Abigail's arm. *"Tell me."*

Abigail gave in. "I lied to and betrayed my entire family."

"You did not."

"Yes." Abigail nodded, looking square into Lisa's eyes. "I did."

"Then wait right here."

Lisa swiftly crossed the patio, helped herself to two glasses of champagne and returned, handing one of them to Abigail.

Abigail took a swallow. "I slept with Zach. He's that guy you just saw. Only, I didn't know he was Zach then."

"You're an adult."

"I know."

"Was it good?"

Abigail shot her an incredulous look. "That's irrelevant."

"Yeah, but was it good?"

"Yes."

"So far I'm not hearing anything particularly problematic."

"Yeah, well, it gets better. He blackmailed me. Threatened to tell Travis and Seth—"

"Tell them what you like in bed?" It was Lisa's turn to be incredulous.

"*No.* No. It was something that I *told* him in bed."

"Oh, good. Though I have to admit, you had me curious." Lisa waggled her brow. "Little Bo Peep outfit, handcuffs, whipped cream."

"Give me a break."

"It's not as if you can tell by looking at a person."

"I'm not into handcuffs."

Lisa shrugged. "So what'd you tell him?"

Abigail was having second thoughts about the conversation. She glossed over the facts. "The important point is that he blackmailed me into helping him get a variance to his water license."

"He *got* a variance?" Working in the mayor's office, Lisa was well aware of the contentious water issues.

Abigail shook her head. "The committee turned him down. And now he wants me to try again."

"Wow, Abby. Unless we're talking black leather and whips, and even then, just tell him no."

"This isn't about kinky sex."

"Then just tell him no."

"There are hundreds of jobs at stake." Abigail found herself defending Zach. "Hundreds of orphans' jobs at stake. Because that's what Zach does. He grew up in foster care, and he's built this whole brewery conglomerate to give jobs to other foster kids. You should see the place, Lisa. The headquarters are in Houston, and the people who work there, well, they all but worship Zach and his partner, Alex. He's given them all a real shot in life, given them a place to belong. And I'm the only person who might be able to help him save it."

"What does this have to do with water?"

"They need to up production at their Craig Mountain brewery. To do that, they need water. If they don't, it all falls apart like a row of dominoes."

"It's still not your problem," Lisa told her gently.

"They're his family."

"And you want to help them."

"I do," Abigail admitted. "I know it'll set a precedent that will hurt the ranchers. But I want to do it anyway."

Lisa smiled. "He must be damn good in bed."

"He is." Abigail felt her cheeks grow warm. "That's irrelevant. But he is."

Lisa's grin widened. "Then you'd better help him."

"And betray my family." That was the conundrum. She might sympathize with Zach, but the facts remained the same.

Lisa linked arms with her. "It's not the worst betrayal in the world. Besides, if they kick you out of the house, I'll take your room."

Abigail tried to smile at the joke, but she couldn't quite pull it off.

"Chill, Abby," said Lisa. "The water battle will go on for a long, long time to come. And in the end, Zach's variance will be a mere blip on the radar."

"*If* I pull it off," Abigail reminded her as they started for the door. Having met some of Zach's employees, she truly wanted to save their jobs. "I honestly don't know what I can do to change the committee's mind."

"Seth told me about all the research you did on this," Lisa reminded her. "The paper you wrote, your presentation in Denver. You didn't let those bureaucrats intimidate you. The Ranchers Association thinks the world of you. He also told me he credits you with getting him elected. You wrote every speech, developed every policy. You've been a straight A student since first grade. You're brilliant, Abby. If anyone can do it, it's you."

Seven

It was after midnight. Having finished a phone call to Alex, Zach moved from the bedroom of his hotel suite to the living room where Abigail was curled up on the sofa, reading her way through one of the papers from the thick rejection file. She still wore the filmy, plum, strapless bridesmaid dress. It draped enticingly across her thighs, highlighting her toned, tanned, sexy legs. Her feet were bare. Her hair had come loose from the updo and now framed her face with those same auburn wisps he'd fallen for the first night he'd met her. Her makeup was slightly smudged, and a hint of cleavage peeked out from her bodice. It was all he could do not to stride across the room and pull her into his arms and kiss her until they couldn't see straight.

He knew she didn't want that. But he also knew she was still attracted to him. And, right now, he wanted it enough for the both of them.

She lifted her gaze to look at him, those golden eyes all but glowing in the soft light from the table lamp.

He knew she'd caught him staring. And he imagined there was no mistaking his thoughts, since he was all but salivating at the thought of her.

But she didn't seem to notice, or else she didn't care. She smiled serenely. "I've got it."

He had to forcibly pull back from the sensual path he'd been on. "Got what?"

"The solution." Smile broadening, she asked, "You got any champagne around here?"

"I can order anything you want."

"You might want to order some champagne."

"Why?" he prompted.

She chuckled softly, coming to her feet. "It's so simple. It was there all along."

He knew she couldn't be talking about sex, but, man, did he wish she was. "What was there all along?"

"You move your company headquarters to Lyndon."

Her words didn't compute into anything logical in his brain, so he didn't respond.

"That's the answer, Zach."

"Is that a joke?" If it was, she was keeping a pretty straight face.

"It's not a joke."

"It's ridiculous." DFB had only recently agreed to a new five-year lease for the office space in Houston. His two-hundred-strong at headquarters had houses there, families there. They were all Texans.

"You do that," she singsonged, obviously ignoring his reaction. "That's over two hundred new jobs in the Lyndon area. Your variance application then has a fundamental impact on employment creation in the region, and you've just earned yourself mandatory exemption."

Against all odds, the woman truly was serious.

"Do you have any idea what it would take to make that kind of move?" he asked. "There are legal and incorporation impacts, taxation impacts, export-licensing impacts, not to mention uprooting two-hundred people and their families."

She sauntered toward him. "I think what you mean to say is, 'You're brilliant, Abigail. Thank you so much for giving me a real solution to an impossible problem'."

He knew she was brilliant, but he couldn't quite wrap his head around the magnitude of her suggestion. His words were confrontational, but his tone was soft. "I believe I mean to say, 'You're insane, Abigail. This will never work in real life'."

She came to a halt in front of him, all soft and sexy and proud. "You coerced me. You blackmailed me. You stalked me."

"How did I stalk you?"

"To the wedding."

He considered that. "Okay. Fair enough."

"And now, after all that, after I practically made my brain bleed thinking this through, you're refusing to take my advice?"

"Your advice is frightening."

"It's brilliant."

"I don't see how it can work."

"It can work." Her eyes took on that glow of intelligence as her brain obviously clicked through a catalog of facts. "Or maybe it can't work. But it's all I've got."

He recognized that it was an extraordinary plan. The only flaw was that it wouldn't work, at least not for him, not for DFB. But that didn't change the fact that she'd been clever to come up with it.

"They tell me you're a genius," he found himself saying.

His words clearly took her by surprise. "Who are they?"

"People I talk to. People in Lyndon. Are you a genius, Abigail?"

"I'm smart enough that you should be listening to me."

"And I'm stupid enough to think there's another way."

"You're not stupid. Exactly."

"Ouch."

"I'd say you were self-confident to a fault."

"It's taken me a long way in life." He felt compelled to defend himself.

"That doesn't mean it shouldn't be mitigated."

"You're really quite fearless, aren't you?"

"Where did that come from?"

"Nobody challenges me like this. Nobody pushes me, nobody

makes me second-guess myself. I've missed you," he confessed, easing closer to her.

"In a good way?"

Was it his imagination or was she leaning slightly toward him?

"My life seems flat when you're not around."

"Mine seems a whole lot simpler when you're not around."

"You want simpler?"

She hesitated, brain obviously cataloging again. Finally she shook her head.

"Neither do I," he muttered. He gave in to impulse and lifted his hand, cupping her cheek, easing his spread fingers into her hair. "I want you."

Her eyes closed, and she turned her face into his palm. "When you touch me," she breathed, "nothing else seems to matter."

"Everything matters," he countered. "But you matter the most."

"Zach…" She sighed. "What now?"

He moved in. "Now I hope I kiss you."

"We shouldn't."

"Agreed. Not the way things have been between us. But you're free from me now. From here on in. No matter what, I'll never bother you again."

"So I can leave? And you won't try to stop me?"

He held his breath, afraid she'd do exactly that. "You can do anything you want."

But she didn't move. In fact, her lips softened and parted, and her pupils dilated ever so slightly.

"Kiss me, Zach."

His arms went around her instantly. He tried to be gentle, but passion pushed him on. He kissed her deeply, holding her tight, reveling in the feel of her body pressed against his own. He'd missed her so much. Every minute of every day they'd been apart, he'd missed her.

She was soft to his hard, supple to his taut steel. She smelled like wildflowers, and she tasted of champagne.

She kissed him back, her delicate hands gripping his shoulders, her tongue tangling with his, opening to him, molding against him. Desire crested in his bloodstream, and he knew he was careening toward losing control. He forced himself to pull back.

"I'm sorry," he rasped. "I didn't mean this to get out of hand."

"It's out of hand?" She was equally breathless, and her hands went to the buttons on his shirt.

"Abby," he warned.

"What?" she asked, glancing up, tone falsely innocent, eyes blinking up at him.

"You're a very smart woman."

"I am," she agreed, still unbuttoning.

"You're unbuttoning my shirt."

"Also true." She separated the fabric and placed a hot kiss on his chest.

"You know what this means."

"In fact, I do."

"Just so we're clear."

"We're clear."

"I can't keep my hands off you."

She smiled impishly up at him. "You're doing a pretty good job so far."

He scooped her into his arms and strode for the bedroom. "Let's fix that."

Her luscious lips went to his neck. "Please do."

He was in the bedroom in seconds, setting her down on the bed, stretching out beside her, kissing her lips, her neck, her shoulders, inhaling deeply as he ran his fingers through her soft hair.

"This is the sexiest dress ever," he told her.

"Katrina picked it."

"Remind me to thank her." He released the zipper and pushed the fabric down over her breasts.

Abby groaned. "I'm trying to picture that conversation."

He kissed one nipple, bringing the tip to a bead.

Her fingertips dug into his shoulders.

"Picturing it now?" he teased.

"Huh?"

"Nothing."

With a free hand he drew her dress up along her bare thighs, reveling in the soft, tender skin, his thumbs drawing circles as he moved higher.

She finished with his buttons, pushing his jacket and shirt off his shoulders. He let them fall to the floor, taking her lips in a deep kiss.

He touched the hot silk of her panties, and she gasped against his mouth. Her panties were filmy, barely there, and he easily pulled them off, down her gorgeous legs, tossing them to the side. In answer, her hands went to his pants, fumbling with the button and his zipper.

He retrieved his wallet, working with one hand for a condom as she pulled down his zipper, grazing him with her knuckles, her hand surrounding him through his boxers.

He followed the contours of her body, reveling in her soft skin, kissing her from her hairline to her toes and back again. Then he finally rose above her, watching her expression, the moue of her pink mouth, the glow of her golden eyes, the sheen of sweat on her forehead, and he gently pushed inside.

He groaned out loud. "How can anything be so good?"

A haze was taking over his brain. A roar had started in his ears. And all nonessential systems were shutting down.

Abigail was the center of his world. The blackmail was done. From this moment on, she had the power.

"Oh, Lucky." She kissed his mouth, wrapped her arms around his neck, tightened her legs around his waist, her entire body cradling his.

He'd never felt anything like it. Explosions started at the base of his brain, growing in intensity, fanning out.

He heard her cry, felt her body ripple around him, and he let himself cascade over the edge.

Their breathing was ragged, and long minutes passed while he held her to him, passion slowly throbbing its way from his body.

Neither spoke. Her body was limp, and her head was tucked into the crook of his neck.

"I thought about what you said," she whispered.

"What did I say?" Whatever it was, he'd say it again.

"About your employees being your family. It made me want to help you. To throw my heart and soul into it."

"Thank you," he said simply.

"You really do need to move your headquarters."

"Can we talk about this later?" Though he accepted that she was right. He and Alex had to sit down and seriously talk about how that might work.

"There is no later," she told him, tone regretful. "I've got a 9:00 a.m. flight."

Stay, his mind screamed. "Back to the ranch?" he asked instead.

She nodded.

Her words made him feel helpless. She didn't want to go back there. She shouldn't have to go back there.

"Have you told them?" he asked, already knowing the answer.

"I'm never going to tell them, Zach. And you can't either."

"You can't live your life for your family."

"You're living yours for your employees."

"That's different." He loved his job. He loved working with Alex, and he took immense satisfaction in the success of Red, White and Brew.

She gave him an ironic smile and cocked her head.

"Hot tub or bed?" he asked, deciding to assume she was staying the night. Before she could refuse, he touched the bottom of her chin with his index finger, placing a gentle kiss on her swollen mouth.

"Bed," he decided for her on a whisper. "Don't make me let go of you just yet."

Wrapped in Zach's discarded dress shirt, sleeves rolled up a few turns, Abigail gazed through the window of the darkened hotel bedroom, watching the distant spot of light that was an early flight taking off from the Denver airport. It trailed across the sky, disappearing into a blend of stars on the horizon. It wouldn't be long before she was on a plane just like that, winging her way north, while Zach made his way south.

She heard him moving behind her, and then his arms were around her, drawing her back against him.

"Hey." His voice was husky above her ear.

"I didn't mean to wake you," she apologized.

"I wasn't asleep."

She drew a breath and allowed herself to absorb his warmth. He seemed so strong, so sure, as if nothing in the world could slow him down. She tried to imagine how he'd become such a successful man, how he'd overcome what must have been innumerable challenges in his childhood.

"What was it like?" she found herself asking.

"What was what like?" he asked.

"Growing up. Alone. In the group home."

"You don't want to hear about that."

She turned in his arms. "Yes, I do."

He gazed at her for a minute, eyes dark, expression serious. "Unremarkable," he finally answered.

That didn't come anywhere near to satisfying her. "Were you happy, sad, lonely?"

"We were all lonely."

She looped her arms loosely around his waist, studying his expression. "I'm trying to imagine what it must have been like when you were little."

"It was like having a hundred brothers."

"But no parents."

"Parents, no. Workers, yes. Around the clock. Some of them stayed for years. Some of them seemed to like me a lot. Well—" he gave a wry smile "—when I was little, anyway. But then I met Alex, and we were typical, active boys, and we mostly made the workers all crazy."

Abigail smiled back, but her heart couldn't help aching for him.

"What about you?" he asked. "What was it like when you were little."

"Seth and Travis were horrible to us girls."

"I can imagine."

"They teased us unmercifully. I was the oldest. Mandy was pretty tough. While Katrina was always really small and delicate. They weren't too bad with her. I guess even as kids, they realized it would be cruel to go after her."

"What did they do to you and Mandy?"

"Everything from putting spiders in our beds to throwing us into the freezing-cold lake in the spring. Travis sneaked into my bedroom once in the middle of the night and glued my hair to my pillow. The next morning, Mom had to cut it off."

Zach smoothed back her hair. "Travis get a whipping?"

"My parents didn't believe in spanking. But he spent the next two weeks shoveling manure in the hot sun."

"Learned his lesson?"

"He never did anything like that again. But I don't think manual labor ever bothered him much."

"At St. Stephen's they had a big old leather strap."

"They beat you?"

"They didn't call it beating back then. They called it discipline."

She cringed just thinking about it. "Did you..."

"Oh, yes."

"Oh, Zach." She put a sympathetic hand to his cheek.

He covered it with his. "It wasn't that bad. Schoolyard fights were worse. But it toughened Alex and me up. By the time we left, there wasn't much the world could throw at us that we couldn't take."

She didn't buy his dismissal. She knew how cruel kids could be, and she'd always had her parents as champions. And she also had her brothers and sisters by her side. Though Seth and Travis would tease them at home, they'd staunchly defended them to any outsiders.

It had been interesting when she started dating.

"Did you go to a local school?" she asked Zach.

"Classes were at St. Stephen's."

"So, boys only."

"Boys only."

"How did you date?"

"We didn't. From about fifteen on, we had supervised out-ings. We sometimes came across girls, at local fairs or movie nights. But it was always in groups, always supervised, never a chance to steal a kiss or cop a feel."

"How'd you learn about sex?" she asked. Somewhere along the way, he'd become awfully good at it.

He grinned. "Hearsay and rumor, and the occasional contra-band girlie magazine."

She smiled along with him. "And how old were you when you left St. Stephen's."

"Eighteen."

"So, how long did it take you to get lucky, Lucky?"

His gaze warmed on her. "A long time. I got very lucky a few weeks ago, in Lyndon, Colorado. With a woman who was ten times more beautiful than anyone I'd ever seen in a magazine."

"Oh, *good answer*," she approved with a nod.

"I mean it."

"You've learned a lot about women along the way, Zach Rainer."

"I'd like to learn more about you."

She sobered. "You've got about two hours."

He drew her closer. "Two hours. And that's it?"

"That's it." She'd been absent from the ranch far too much since the election. It wasn't fair to Travis. And for the next week, they were also helping to take care of the Terrell place next to theirs while Caleb and Reed were on their honeymoons with Mandy and Katrina. She couldn't afford even one more day in Denver.

Back in Houston, two hours after his plane had landed, Zach sat across the boardroom table from Alex.

"You're serious," Alex stated unnecessarily.

"You don't think I've come at this from every possible angle?"

Alex drummed his fingers rhythmically on the tabletop. "And you trust her?"

"What's not to trust? There's nothing in this for her."

"It gets you to Lyndon."

"I don't think she wants me in Lyndon." Zach could get big-headed about this and decide that Abigail had some interest in him beyond their brief fling. But he was realistic. Her goodbye this morning had been final.

Not that he blamed her. He'd forced her to go against her family. And if he knew anything about Abby, it was that she was loyal to the core. Though their lovemaking was explosive, it was temporary and in some ways selfish. She wasn't going to let herself do that again.

Alex leaned back in his chair, twirling a silver pen between his fingers. "Then I guess we get the legal department assembled this afternoon."

"And Accounting," said Zach. "Relocating is going to be expensive. We'll have to break our lease. I can't imagine what it'll do to our taxes. And we should offer employees some kind of moving allowance."

"Are there even enough houses for everybody in Lyndon, Colorado?"

Zach realized it was a good question. "I wonder if we could stage it out, maybe plan the bulk of the move for next summer. That way, people with kids wouldn't be so inconvenienced."

"You think people will quit?"

"Some might," Zach reasoned. "But at least they'll have the option."

Alex's frown deepened. "You are absolutely sure there's no other way?"

"I am absolutely sure." He'd had three of their lawyers look over the moratorium and Abigail's suggestion. They proclaimed her a genius and told Zach they'd hire her as a researcher in a heartbeat.

"There is a bright side," said Alex.

"Yeah?"

"I'm starting to think Stephanie might have been bluffing."

"Will you take her back?" Zach was often baffled by his friend's relationship with his girlfriend Stephanie. It seemed to cause him a whole lot more angst than happiness.

When she wasn't angry, she was pouting. She demanded nearly all his attention. If he was half an hour late leaving the office, she was on the phone. And when he traveled on business, she was always convinced he was going to spend time with other women.

"I don't want her back," said Alex. "But she does have her ways. I figure it's safer if I leave the state. I'll go be the advance man in Colorado. Keep me away from temptation."

"I don't understand how you can possibly be tempted."

"That's because you've never been in love."

Zach might not have ever been in love, but he couldn't imagine love was anything like Alex and Stephanie's relationship. If a guy was going to go to all the trouble to be with one woman, she should at least make him happy. A vision of Abigail flashed through his mind. Okay, he wouldn't exactly call every moment with her happy. Exhilarating, yes. Exciting, absolutely. And the highs were very, very high. But the lows sure sucked.

Then again, the lows were mostly when she left him.

"It's not all laughs and sunshine," Alex put in.

"Apparently not."

"The good is very good."

"And the bad is very bad." Zach shifted his mind back to Alex and Stephanie. "Seems to me it should at least be a fifty-fifty proposition to make it worth a guy's while."

"It'll happen to you one day."

"Not like Stephanie."

"Yeah, well." Alex brought his hands down on the arms of his chair. "Stephanie ain't going to happen for me either. To make sure of that, I'm going to Colorado."

"No forwarding address?"

"Probably for the best." Alex stretched. "Damn, this is going to be expensive."

"That it is," Zach agreed. "Only thing it's got going for it is that's it's better than the alternative."

"True enough."

Zach started to rise, but Alex spoke again.

"So, you going to call her?"

"Abigail?"

Alex set his pen down on the table. "Yes, Abigail. The woman you slept with last night."

"I never said I slept with her."

"Are you going to call her?"

"No." Zach would like to call her. He'd love to call her. But he'd bothered her enough for one lifetime. It was time to back off.

"You mind if I call her?" asked Alex.

"What for?"

"To ask her out."

Zach's fingers curled tightly around the arms of his chair. "On a *date?*"

"There's got to be some kind of nightlife in Lyndon."

"Over my dead body."

"So she's off limits?"

Zach leaned forward. "Look me in the eye, Alex. What do you see?"

"My body chopped up into tiny little pieces if I so much as look sideways at Abigail Jacobs."

"Close enough."

"But you're not going to call her."

Zach wished he could. "She doesn't want to hear from me."

"Got a minute?" Lisa's head popped up above the roofline of the shed where Abigail was perched while she replaced some broken shingles. Seth was perpetually busy on civic matters in Lyndon. Mandy and Caleb were honeymooning in Hawaii. Katrina and Reed had opted for Australia. Abigail's parents were staying in Denver for a while, to be close to the medical facilities while her father completed his recovery. As expected, Travis and Abigail were left holding the fort.

Ozzy gave a belated, warning bark from his post at the bottom of the ladder.

"I didn't know you were coming today." Abigail pulled a couple of roofing nails out of her mouth and dropped them back in the pouch on her leather tool belt.

"Drove in with Seth." Lisa stepped up two more rungs and maneuvered herself around the top of the ladder.

"Careful," Abigail cautioned. She was wearing heavy, leather work boots with thick-tread soles, while Lisa sported a pair of expensive pumps.

Lisa's gauzy, pastel-patterned blouse billowed in the breeze above her skinny jeans. "Wow. Quite the view up here."

Abigail glanced around. She'd been focused on work for the past few hours, but now she noted the fall colors against the evergreens and newly snowcapped peaks in the nearby foothills. October was well under way, and they could expect the first snowfall in a few weeks.

Lisa sat down next to her on the sun-warmed, black shingles. "How's it going?"

Abigail shrugged. "Busy." Fall was a frantic time on the ranch. Along with roundup, they had to make sure everything was winterized and battened down. Colorado was a beautiful state, but it had its fair share of rain and snow. "How about you?"

"Busy in Lyndon, too. We're knee-deep in next year's budget. The environmentalists have turned the Canada goose into a poster child, and the flocks are wreaking havoc at the airport. You know, the usual."

Abigail scooted backward on her canvas work pants, setting another shingle strip in place.

"Saw an interesting application at city hall today," said Lisa, swiping her hair back from her face as the wind raced up the pitch of the roof.

Abigail hammered in the first nail.

"For a business license," Lisa continued. "Corporate headquarters of DFB Incorporated."

Abigail hit her finger with the hammer. "Ouch!"

"It's the parent company for Craig Mountain Brewery."

"I know who they are." Abigail shook the pain out of her hand, her mind reeling. Zach was going to do it. It had been three weeks since she'd presented her idea, and she hadn't heard a word about his decision.

"Did Zach tell you he was doing this?"

"He didn't."

"But it was your idea," Lisa guessed.

"It was," Abigail admitted, taking a breath and setting the next nail.

"It was absolutely brilliant."

It had been a brilliant idea. But it was also a very radical idea.

"I didn't think he'd actually go through with it. He's uprooting more than two hundred people."

"The water license exemption was attached to the business application."

Abigail looked up. "So it's signed, sealed and delivered?"

She wanted to ask if Lisa had seen Zach, if he was in town. But she forced herself to stay silent. He knew full well where she was, and how to get hold of her. The fact that he hadn't bothered contacting her told her everything she needed to know.

"They want to take over the Buskell Building on Fourth. That means a variance to zoning, and they'll need to make provisions for parking. But all that's minor stuff compared to the water license."

"So he's really doing it."

"Looks like."

Abigail let the hammer rest on the roof, gazing across the river, trying hard not to remember her last night with Zach.

"What did he have on you?" Lisa asked softly.

"It's not important."

"You look sad."

Abigail mustered a smile. "I'm not sad. Dad's doing better. Mandy and Katrina are having fantastic honeymoons. The price of beef is up."

"You can't fool me." Lisa scooted closer. "I know you too well."

"You've only known me for five months." Ironic, really, considering Abigail's own family hadn't picked up on anything being wrong.

"It's the genetic link. You have my eyes. And they're sad."

"Your eyes are green and round. Mine are hazel and almond shaped."

"What did he have on you, Abby?"

"You're like a broken record." But deep down inside, Abigail wanted to share with someone.

Lisa leaned back on the heels of her hands. "I'll just wait."

"Okay." Abigail set up for another strip of shingles, then another and another, moving farther away from Lisa, while her mind went to war with itself.

Finally, she dropped the hammer and rested her hands on her upraised knees. "Fine," she called out.

"Yeah?" Lisa called back.

"Yeah."

Lisa stood up, made her way across the roof then plopped back down again.

"Cone of silence?" Abigail asked.

"Always."

"I told him I didn't like working on the ranch." There. She'd said it out loud.

Lisa drew back in obvious surprise. "You don't?"

The rest of the words seemed to leap out. "I loved the campaign. I like the city. I like office work. I like power lunches and research and analysis."

"So, why are you here? You could get a hundred jobs in Lyndon or anywhere else."

"Because they need me. The family needs me."

"No, they—"

"They need me," Abigail repeated with certainty.

Lisa was silent for a long moment. "Yeah, I guess they do."

"If I was going to say something—" Abigail plucked at a seam on the leather belt "—I should have done it sooner. But now Seth's gone, and Mom and Dad bought that condo in Palm Springs, and Mandy's up at the Terrells, and Katrina was never here in the first place." She drew a breath. "And I can't abandon Travis."

"So, you're going to stay here forever?"

"Not forever. But until something changes, yes. Maybe Travis will find a wife. Maybe she'll love ranching. Maybe they'll have sons or daughters who want to take over."

Lisa shook her hair so that it was blowing back from her face. "That sounds like a pretty long-term proposition."

"It does," Abigail agreed. But hoping something would come along to change the circumstances was all she had right now. She couldn't change the circumstances herself. It all depended on external forces.

"Wish I could help," Lisa offered. "But I don't know a heifer from a milk cow."

Abigail chuckled. "You're helping Seth."

"Seth's doing a great job."

"I know he is." Abigail hesitated, desperate to ask about Zach, but not wanting to give Lisa the wrong idea. Or maybe asking would give Lisa exactly the right idea, since Abigail had pretty much been obsessing about him since Denver.

"The business license," she ventured. "Was it…submitted locally?"

"Are you asking whether Zach's in town?"

"Yes." There didn't seem to be any point in denying it, especially to Lisa, who seemed to have an uncanny knack for figuring things out.

"I take it you have feelings for him?"

Abigail shook her head in denial, more for her own benefit than Lisa's. "I slept with him, so…you know…it's weird. If I'm going to run into him, I'd like to brace myself."

"The application was signed by someone named Alex Cable."

"That's Zach's business partner." So, no Zach. Just as well. The last thing in the world she needed was to see him again.

Eight

Zach almost didn't see the guy as he wheeled his Jaguar around the corner on the dark Colorado highway, setting the car up for the turnoff to Craig Mountain. But there he was, hood to his pickup truck propped open, leaning inside in the drizzling rain, feet planted carelessly on the side of the road where somebody could easily clip his legs.

Zach hit the brakes, bringing his car to a halt behind the pickup. He put it in neutral, set the park brake, and left his lights on so nobody else would miss seeing the vehicles. Then he exited his Jag, hiking his suit collar up against the rainy weather.

"Need some help?" he called, extracting his cell phone from his jacket pocket. Hopefully, the cowboy was registered with the auto club.

"I think I've— Ouch! Crap." It was a female voice. "Got it."

He came around the end of the hood. "Abigail?"

She twisted her head to stare incredulously up at him in the gloom.

"What happened?" he asked, keeping his voice even, trying not to react to the shock of seeing her again. She had a grease smudge on her cheek. Her clothes were worn and muddy. And the battered hat on her head was dripping with rainwater.

She'd never looked more gorgeous.

He had to force himself to gaze down into the engine.

"I replaced the fan belt," she informed him, voice unsteady.

But then his eyes focused on a spreading dark patch on her bare forearm. "You're bleeding!" He reflexively reached for her, but then abruptly stopped himself, not wanting to hurt her any further.

She lifted her injured arm and dispassionately inspected the wound. "It'll stop."

"What do you mean, it'll stop?" A stream of blood was trickling off her elbow onto the engine.

"Do you mind cranking the key?"

"Abigail."

"You don't want to help?"

"You've been injured."

"Fine." She extracted herself from under the hood, setting a wrench on the fender and turning for the driver's door. "I'll do it myself."

"Get into my car," he commanded, checking his cell phone, finding no signal.

She kept walking. "The truck will start now."

He followed. "You need medical attention."

"Don't be melodramatic." She opened the door and twisted her arm to get a better look in the glow of the dome light. "A few butterfly bandages will do the trick."

The wound was even worse than he thought. "I am not letting you drive like this."

She swung into the driver's seat. "It's not your decision."

He quickly snagged the key from the ignition.

"Hey," she protested.

Ozzy popped to his feet in the passenger seat and barked once, then wagged his tail at Zach and clambered onto Abigail's lap to get closer.

"Give me back the keys, Zach."

Zach scratched the dog's head. "What's he doing here?"

"He likes road trips. Now give me the keys."

"Not a chance." There was no way in the world he was sending her out injured on a dark, rainy highway.

She gripped the wheel with her good hand, glaring at him in anger. But her mouth was also tense with pain, white at the edges, and sweat had beaded on her forehead. "You can't do this to me."

"What the hell are you trying to prove?" he demanded.

"Nothing."

"That you're tough? Fine. I believe you're tough."

"I'm not trying to prove a thing to you. I couldn't care less what you think of me. I'm trying to get these supplies to the ranch."

He scooped Ozzy from her lap and tucked the pup against his chest. "Not tonight you're not."

She leaned back. "Zach, stop it."

He put his free hand on her shoulder, and tried to keep his voice gentle. "This truck is a stick shift."

"So what?"

"So you need both hands to drive it."

"I have both hands."

"We're thirty minutes from the hospital in Lyndon, or thirty minutes from the paramedic at the Craig Mountain construction site. Which is it going to be?"

"I'm going back to the ranch."

"We're two hours from the ranch."

"There is no we."

"There is right now." Giving up completely on logic and reason, he pocketed her keys, paced back around the front of the truck and slammed the hood with finality. He swore the woman had lost her mind.

He returned to find her eyes closed, teeth gritted, arm limp by her side. Her cheeks had gone a shade paler.

"I'm taking you to the hospital," he announced, trying to figure out how to force her into his car without hurting her.

"Craig Mountain," she retorted, opening her eyes, glaring in defiance.

Fine with him. The job-site paramedic was highly qualified.

"I'm sure they'll have some morphine for the pain and a local anesthetic for the stitches."

She coughed a cold laugh. "I'm a cowboy. All I need is an aspirin and some alcohol."

"For rubbing or ingesting?"

"A little of both."

Impressed by her attempt at humor, he braced his hand firmly beneath her arm. "Come on, partner."

"I'll bleed all over your Jaguar."

"That's why they invented detailing shops."

She eased her way out of the cab. "I don't need stitches."

"How about we let the medical professionals decide that."

"You are so stubborn." But the fight was gone from her voice.

"Yeah," he drawled. "I'm the stubborn one."

They made their way to his running vehicle, and he settled her into the passenger seat, placing Ozzy on the small backseat behind her. Glancing at her arm made him grimace. She had to be in a whole lot of pain.

"This is completely unnecessary," she complained.

"Humor me." He stripped off his suit jacket, tossed it back next to Ozzy. Then he began unbuttoning his cotton shirt.

"What are you— Oh, seriously, Zach. It can wait till we get to the castle."

"I don't think so." He doffed the shirt, bent on one knee and loosely wrapped it over her arm.

"Ever think of becoming a nurse?" she asked.

"Not until now."

"You're very gentle."

"You're very brave."

"It's just a scratch." But she was beginning to shiver.

"Cold?" he asked, worried that it might be a sign of shock.

"Little bit."

He set her arm in her lap then retrieved his jacket, draping it around her shoulders. He turned the heater dial to full, softly latching the door before rounding the hood to get into the driver's side.

"So, how've you been?" he asked as he eased out the clutch and pulled onto the dark highway. "I mean, up until now."

"Fine," she answered, sounding a lot more frustrated than faint. Maybe she wasn't going into shock. "And you?"

"Busy. I guess you must have heard?"

"That you wised up and took my advice? Yes, I had heard that."

"When you're right, you're right," he allowed.

He took the first few turns of the mountain road.

"So you're moving to Lyndon?"

He couldn't identify the emotion in her voice. And, under the circumstances, maybe he was foolish to try. But he would love to know if his moving made her happy? Sad? Ticked off? If she was ticked off, she had no one to blame but herself. It was her idea.

"I am," he told her.

"When did you get to town?"

"Today. Alex has been here for a while. He's taking care of setting up the new head office in Lyndon. I've got some work to do at Craig Mountain."

The pavement abruptly ended, and he hit a pothole on the gravel stretch.

Abigail hissed in a pained breath.

"Sorry."

"No big deal. I also heard it was official. You got the water-license exemption."

Zach was sure the jolt had caused her considerable pain, but there seemed little point in arguing. Maybe discussing his business would take her mind off the injury. "Your plan worked like a charm," he told her. "Thanks for the help."

"No problem."

He couldn't help chuckling at that. "That's not what you said a few weeks ago."

"I'm over it."

"I'm glad to hear that."

She shrugged. "In the end, you made it easy. It was nothing

I said or did. An exemption is an exemption. Anybody could have gotten one by bringing in two hundred jobs."

"I wouldn't have known about the exemption, if not for you."

She cast a sidelong glance his way. "But we're still keeping that our secret, right?"

"Right."

"Along with everything else? There's no expiration date on a blackmail payoff," she confirmed.

"I said yes."

"Just so we're clear."

"We're clear." He paused. "But I didn't think there were official rules for blackmail."

"Honor among thieves."

"We're not thieves."

"We'd've been good at it, though."

He chuckled.

"Trickery, subterfuge, deception and clandestine meetings."

"We'd also have to steal something," he pointed out.

She leaned her head back. "I don't need anything."

"Except medical attention."

"Do we need to steal it?"

"We do not." He nodded out through the windshield. "See those lights up ahead?"

She squinted. "Way up in the trees?"

"They're farther up the mountain. That's the new building for Craig Mountain. The walls are up. The roof is on. And it'll be clad to weather by the end of the week."

"Congratulations."

"There's a long way to go. But so far we're on schedule."

"Did you decide whether or not to do a restaurant?"

He pretty much had, but he hadn't made if official yet. "I'm not sure," he hedged, to keep the conversation going. "What do you think I should do?"

She got a faraway look in her eyes, and her tone softened. "I think people would love to have dinner at the castle."

"Yeah?" he prompted. "Why?"

"It's beautiful, for one thing. And the place has enormous

potential. If I was you, I'd take a bunch of that stuff out of the towers, polish it up and use it to decorate the restaurant."

"Anything in particular?"

"Whatever you want. The paintings, for one thing. The furniture. There were some awesome silver pieces up there, and the dishes. Did you see the dishes?"

Her growing enthusiasm surprised him. He hadn't paid much attention to the stuff in the towers. "Will you show me what you mean?"

"Sure. Seriously, Zach. It could be as much a museum as a restaurant. Imagine the experience you could conjure up for guests. Costumed staff, vintage dishes." She gave an impish grin. "Flagons of mead and ale served by lusty wenches."

He grinned. "I like the way you're thinking."

"You just like the lusty wenches."

"No. I have a thing for your brain."

"Once word got around, the restaurant would practically market itself."

"I'm sold," he told her.

She waved him off. "You don't have to humor me. I'm only suggesting you think about it."

"I have thought about it." He gave in to impulse. "Help me plan it. Help me design it."

She scoffed out a laugh. "Yeah, right."

"Why not?"

"I don't have time."

"What? You need to herd more cows? Shovel more manure? Repair more engines?"

His anger bubbled up as he was reminded of her injured arm. What kind of family sent her out on the highway all alone at night? What was she doing repairing a pickup truck by the side of the road? What the hell else was she up to on the ranch? Bronc riding? Bullfighting?

"Don't go there," she warned.

He gripped the steering wheel, but held his tongue, concentrating on choosing the smoothest path through a series of potholes.

The silence stretched.

"When you're right, you're right," he finally allowed.

Now, if only she'd be smart enough to figure out what was right for her. She was obviously still working as a ranch hand. And she was obviously exhausted by it. There were fatigue lines around her eyes, and she looked thinner than he remembered.

She hadn't deserved to get hurt today. And she shouldn't have been hauling freight on a dark highway in a pickup truck. She had so much more potential than that. And if she wasn't in so much pain, he'd tell her so.

"I apologize. Please show me what you liked in the towers. I won't pressure you. I'll simply take any and all advice you care to give."

She eyed him with suspicion. "Are you being nice because I'm hurt?"

"No."

She pursed her lips in obvious disbelief.

"I'm being nice because I'm nice."

"You are not."

"Am too," he retorted in a childish voice.

"You're a meanie," she mocked.

"You're a tomboy."

She sobered, glancing dubiously down at her dirty jeans. "Okay, well, you're right about that."

He was hit with a sudden jolt of guilt. Why was he picking on her? "You're also very beautiful," he corrected himself.

"Oh, don't kid-glove me, Zach. I'm not hurt all that bad."

"Well, you really are all that beautiful."

"I'm covered in grease."

"Doesn't matter. It's not something you can hide with grease."

She shifted in her seat, grimacing and cradling her arm. "Can we stop arguing?"

"Absolutely."

"I mean it."

"I'm *agreeing* with you."

"Okay." But her tone was cautious.

"Take a look up there." He nodded through the windshield

again, to where the lights were growing stronger through the trees. "Wait till you see how much work they've done on the brewery."

Abigail had tried to convince Zach to take her on a quick tour of the impressive new building. But he was adamant that they go directly to the medical trailer and let somebody look at her arm.

Despite herself, by the time the paramedic finished cleaning her up, she was feeling woozy. She'd said yes to the stitches, but no to the painkillers. After the medic finished, her forearm was covered in a thick layer of gauze and also a thin plastic bag to keep it dry. Zach escorted her to his suite in the castle and insisted she take a hot shower. When she looked in the mirror, she realized why.

Her hair was full of dirt and specks of rust from the inside of the truck's hood. Her hands and face were smeared with grease, while her clothes were damp and dusty.

"Wow," she whispered to her reflection. "Way to impress the guy, Abby."

Then she shook her head at the hopelessness of the situation. What did she care what she looked like in front of him? He knew she was a cowboy, and all they ever did was fight. And it wasn't as though he'd even bothered to tell her he was coming to town. No. They were living different lives again. She was focused on her family, and he was focused on his. Difference was, she understood his commitment. He absolutely refused to see the worth of hers.

Good to know where she stood.

Then again, for now, it would also be good to get clean. Wallowing in self-pity wasn't going to get her anywhere.

She twisted on the ancient taps and stripped off her clothes. She was careful of the water, washing her hair and scrubbing her face with one hand, while holding the other up, out of the stream. The hot water helped ease some of the tension from her body. And she was thinking about what to tell Travis as she dried awkwardly off and wrapped herself in Zach's voluminous, cream-colored robe.

She combed through her wet hair and stepped out of the bathroom, directly into the small living area.

"She wouldn't let me take her to the hospital," Zach was saying into his phone. He sat in an armchair, Ozzy on his lap.

Abigail moved to the small Queen Anne sofa next to him, frowning as she sat down. Who was he talking to about her?

"Not tonight, for sure," he said.

"Who is that?" she mouthed.

"Travis," Zach mouthed silently in return.

Her eyes went wide. "What?" she hissed. Why had he called Travis? *How* had he called Travis?

"You want to talk to her?" Zach asked into the phone. Then he paused. "Sure." He rose and held out the phone, her phone, she realized. That explained how he got the number.

"What did you do?" she muttered as she reached for it.

"Let him know you weren't dead," Zach whispered back.

She glared at Zach while she moved the phone to her ear.

"Travis," she chirped in a cheerful voice.

"You okay?" asked her brother from the other end of the line.

"Perfect."

"How's the arm?"

"Couple of stitches. No big deal."

Zach frowned, and she waggled her finger at him to warn him off.

"Good to hear," said Travis. "I guess you're not coming home tonight."

Abigail glanced at the clock on the mantel. It was nearly ten. "Tomorrow," she told her brother.

"I can send someone for the truck."

"Not necessary. I can drive it home in the morning."

"You sure?"

"I'm sure." With the topical anesthetic wearing off, her arm was beginning to throb, but it would take more than that for her to go into damsel-in-distress mode. "Sorry if Zach exaggerated," she told Travis.

"It was good to get the information."

"I would have called you myself," she said, more for Zach's benefit than hers.

"He was just being neighborly."

"Right." If Travis had any idea just how neighborly Zach had been with her in the past, this would be an entirely different conversation.

"You sure you're okay?" Travis asked.

"Perfect. I'll talk to you in the morning."

"Bye, Abby."

She pressed the end button with her thumb. "Why did you do that?" she asked Zach.

"I thought it would be one less thing for you to worry about." His gaze was steady, sincere.

"You weren't worried he was still ticked off at you?"

Zach shook his head. "You said it yourself. It was an exemption. That rule applies to everyone. And your brother doesn't know you helped me." Zach paused, his expression inscrutable. "Travis thinks he won our last fight, and I went away."

She thought about taking Zach to task again for making her lie to her family, but she honestly didn't have the energy. The throbbing in her arm was growing worse. She wished she'd said yes to the painkillers the medic offered. "Travis thought you were being neighborly."

"I am. How's your arm?"

"It's fine." She set the phone down on an end table, resisting the urge to cradle her injury. She hoped it didn't keep her awake tonight.

"I won't think any less of you because you feel pain, you know."

"I know that."

"Good. Then let's try that again. Abby, how's your arm?"

"It's sore," she admitted, tossing back her damp hair and raising her chin. "Can we move on now?"

He gave what looked like a reluctant smile. "Yeah. We can move on. Shot of whiskey, cowboy?"

"Sure. Why not."

He rose smoothly to his feet. "I've got a thirty-year-old Glen-livet." He opened a cupboard in the small kitchen alcove. "That ought to be in keeping with the theme of our surroundings."

It sounded good to Abigail. She hoped he made it a double.

"On the rocks?" he asked, setting two short, crystal glasses on the countertop.

"Please."

The ice cubes clinked, and the cork made a hollow popping sound as he pulled it out of the bottle. She watched as he poured the amber liquid over the small ice cubes. It looked like at least a double. Good. That would help her sleep.

He lifted both glasses and turned. "Do you think it would compromise beer sales if we were to offer scotch whiskey at the restaurant?"

"I think most customers would like to have the choice," she answered.

"Me, too." He handed her one of the glasses then sat back down in the armchair. "I liked your idea about flagons of ale. I think we could do a lot with a historic theme." He swirled his glass and inhaled appreciatively. Then he took a first sip.

Abigail followed suit. The liquid burned her throat, but in a good way, and she appreciated the warmth that radiated out into her bloodstream. She took a second sip. This was going to feel very good on her arm.

"Alex has always been a bit of a scotch aficionado," Zach continued. "He got me into it, too. There's no reason why we couldn't make that a specialty, maybe do a bit of recon through Scotland, check out some of the lesser-known distilleries, the rarer brands."

Abigail found herself nodding. What a fantastic job that would be. And what a fun addition to the restaurant. She took another sip. It had taken her a while to develop a taste for scotch, but now that she had, she found it a very satisfying and civilized beverage.

"If you feel up to it tomorrow, will you help me hunt through the upper floors?"

"I have to get back to the ranch." Though, at the moment, driving the stick shift didn't sound very appealing.

"A hundred different people can drive the truck to the ranch," said Zach. "You're the only one who has a vision for my restaurant."

Though she knew he was only being kind, her heart warmed at the compliment. She did have a vision for his restaurant. At least, she had a vision that she liked. There was no way to know if anyone else would like it. Staying definitely sounded more appealing than going.

Then again, staying anywhere lately sounded more appealing to her than going home to the ranch. She didn't know whether she'd become spoiled or lazy. But she needed to get past that.

"I really have to go home," she told him, knowing there was a trace of apology in her tone.

"Let's play it by ear." He swirled his drink.

Good enough.

She knew she wasn't going to change her mind, but she could always tell him that in the morning.

She lifted her glass to her lips and realized she'd emptied it.

"Went down good?" he asked.

"Too good," she acknowledged.

"Refill?"

She shook her head. She was already pleasantly woozy, and more than a little tired.

"You want to lie down?"

"I should try to sleep," she admitted, coming to her feet. "Down the hall?" she asked, remembering there were a couple of smaller bedrooms between the suite and the back staircase.

He rose with her. "Take my bed."

"Oh, no, no, no." She shook her head.

"Give me a break. I mean you should sleep in it alone. You've got the bathroom here, and it's comfortable—"

"I'll be fine anywhere. I've slept beside campfires and in line shacks half my life."

He moved toward her. "Good for you. But not when you're hurt. And not on my watch."

"I'm not made of spun glass, Zach."

"Really? Could have fooled me, cowboy." His arm encircled her shoulder. "What with all your pouting, impatience and temper tantrums."

"Stop mocking me."

He urged her away from the couch, while Ozzy settled himself in the warm spot she'd left behind. "Humor me. Please. I'll feel like a cad if I send you to a cold bedroom down the hall while I snuggle in here."

She couldn't help chuckling. "Snuggle?"

Once he had her walking, he steered her to the bed. "Yes. I want you to snuggle." He pulled back the covers.

"Fine," she reluctantly agreed. She was here. She was tired. She was sore. If he was going to insist, she'd bloody well sleep in his bed.

She sat down on the crisp sheet, and the robe slipped off her knee. After a moment, she was aware of Zach's still silence. She glanced up at him.

"What happened?" he demanded.

She followed the direction of his gaze, coming to a purple, half-healed bruise on the middle of her thigh.

"Oh, that." She covered it up with the robe. "I was painting the other day. I tripped halfway down the ladder and smacked into one of the rails."

"You were painting a house?"

"A shed."

"And you fell down a ladder?"

"It wasn't a big deal." Embarrassed that he was going to think she was a hopeless klutz, she pulled her legs up onto the bed, curling them under the covers.

"And this?" he asked.

Too late, she realized the robe had fallen off her shoulder. Zach's thumb traced a barely visible bruise on the tip.

"Pulling a horseshoe."

"Oh, Doll-Face." He sighed.

Before she knew what was happening, he'd leaned in and kissed the fading bruise.

"Zach," she warned.

"Scoot over."

They couldn't do this. *She* couldn't do this. No matter how much she might think she wanted to do this.

"I can't," she managed to say.

"That's not what I meant. You're hurt. You're tired. You're a little drunk."

"I'm not drunk."

"I gave you a lot of scotch."

"It helped."

"That was the point."

"But I'm not drunk."

"I just want to hold you." He eased her to the middle of the bed. "Just for a few minutes."

"Why?" she asked with suspicion, holding herself stiff.

He stretched out beside her. "I don't know." He circled an arm around her, but stopped before he touched her. "Any other sore spots I should know about?"

"My ribs," she answered before she thought it through. She probably should have kept that to herself.

His expression darkened. "What happened to your ribs?"

"I came off a horse. It happens a lot."

He closed his eyes for a long second, but then his arm curled ever so gently around her stomach. "It never happens to me."

She couldn't help smiling at that. The warmth of his arm felt very good against her stomach. As her body relaxed, he put his own head down on the pillow.

"You need to find a safer job," he muttered.

"I need to find someone who won't fight with me all the time."

"Can't argue with that."

"Well, *there's* a first."

Abigail awoke in Zach's arms. There was no way to tell how long he'd stayed with her last night. The whiskey had put her into a sound sleep, and this morning he was showered and changed, lying on top of the quilt, while she was tucked underneath it.

"Morning," he intoned in a deep, lazy voice, smoothing her hair back from her forehead.

"What time is it?" She stifled a yawn.

"Nearly nine."

"Nine?" She started to sit up, but a jolt of pain shot through her arm. She gritted her teeth, just barely controlling an outburst. "I have to call Travis."

"I already did."

"Excuse me?" She must have misunderstood.

"I called Travis. He's sending someone out to the highway to pick up the truck."

Abigail struggled to a sitting position, using her good arm to hold the covers across her chest where the robe had come open while she slept. "You had no right to do that."

"You're definitely in no shape to drive home."

She groaned out a frustrated exclamation.

"Hungry?" he asked.

"I don't even know what to say to that."

"Yes?"

"Since when did you become Travis's best friend?"

"I told him about the stitches."

"He already knew I had stitches."

"You downplayed it. And we agreed it would be better for you to wait a day or two before going back to work."

"What is *wrong* with you?"

"He offered to come and pick you up, but I told him I'd make sure you got home."

"Seriously, Zach. You can't just up and plan another person's life."

"I consulted your family," he defended with a straight face.

"That's not the point."

"You've always made it clear their opinion was important."

"Oh no you don't." She shook her head vigorously. She wasn't about to let him use her family against her. She might love and respect them, but that didn't mean Zach got to do an end run around her own wishes.

He moved to a sitting position, swinging his legs so that his feet rested on the floor. Then he twisted back to look at her. "Do you really want to go home right away?"

Part of her did, and part of her didn't. There was always plenty of bookwork for her to do at the ranch. So she could rest up for a couple of days and still be useful. Then again, Zach had her enthusiastic about the restaurant, and it would be fun to prowl through the castle for a few hours.

"This afternoon would be fine, I guess."

He smiled at that. "I washed your clothes."

Okay, that embarrassed her. "Really?"

"They're on the counter in the bathroom." He stood. "I'll go get us some breakfast. You need anything else? A couple of painkillers?"

"Some aspirin would be nice."

"I can get you something stronger."

"What are you, my dealer?"

He chuckled at that. "I'm just trying to make you comfortable."

She realized that he was. She was the one being surly and antagonistic. All the poor man had done was rescue her from the side of the road, get her medical attention, inform her family and take care of her truckload of ranch supplies, while she was doing nothing but give him grief.

"Aspirin will be fine," she told him, determining to do her best to help him gather some ideas for the restaurant. It was the least she could do to pay him back.

"See you in a couple of minutes."

He left the room with Ozzy at his heels, and by the time she'd freshened up and gotten dressed, the pair of them were back, Zach carrying a tray of coffee and two stacks of delicious-smelling pancakes.

"Where did you get all this?" she asked, taking a seat at the small table. There were two aspirin tablets sitting next to a glass of orange juice, and she popped them into her mouth and washed them down.

"There's a kitchen in the staff area. Staff members do some cooking for lunches and things, since we're so far from any services up here. But, in this case, I got the food from the catering truck set up for the construction site." He sat down across from her, pouring syrup onto his plate of pancakes. "You need any help?"

She bit back the sarcastic retort that formed on her tongue. What was the matter with her? "I'm fine," she answered pleasantly.

He waited a moment before responding. "Good."

"Would you still like some help picking out furniture and things to decorate the restaurant?"

"Absolutely. But only if we don't wear you out."

"You won't wear me out." She cut into her pancakes with the side of her fork, spearing a bite. She'd skipped dinner last night, planning to eat once she got back to the ranch. But after the breakdown, there hadn't been an opportunity. So, this morning, she was famished.

They ate companionably, talking about housing, schools and services available in Lyndon. Abigail had a hard time wrapping her head around the fact that DFB headquarters was moving to Lyndon. And hearing Zach talk, she realized just how complex an undertaking it would be. They had lawyers, accountants and real estate agents working overtime. It was a major disruption to the lives of all his employees.

Listening, she found herself feeling guilty for having pushed the move on him. Then again, there really wasn't another solution to expand Craig Mountain Brewery. And if the expansion was as important as Zach made it out to be, then she'd provided the only solution possible.

They finished breakfast and headed for the north tower. She'd already been up in the center tower. It was easily accessed by a half flight of stairs from the fourth floor. The north tower was a little tougher to access. They made their way to the rear service area, where they came to a narrow, curving, stone staircase that spiraled up in a dim passage. Ozzy gazed up the stairs as if considering his options, then, evidently having decided to skip the climb, settled on a worn, padded bench seat in the stream of sunshine from a recessed window. He wasn't the most athletic dog in the world.

"You're not planning to imprison me up here, are you?" Abigail couldn't help joking as she and Zach made their way up.

"It'd be perfect for that, wouldn't it?" he said over his shoulder.

"If you ever had a fantasy about being an evil count, this would definitely be the place to act it out."

"Scream as loud as you like, sweet darling," he intoned in a dramatic, dire voice. "No one will ever hear you."

"I wonder why they built it this way." She couldn't see any particular use for a room this inaccessible.

"According to Lucas, Lord Ashton modeled the entire castle after one his family owned back in Britain."

"Either that, or he had a crazy wife he needed to imprison."

"That would be my second guess." Zach stopped at the top of the steep staircase, bracing his shoulder against a thick, rough-hewn, oak door.

"I hope she's not still in there," Abigail joked as the hinges squeaked.

"I don't think anyone's been up here in fifty years," said Zach.

"Seriously?" Now she was really curious.

"I'm joking. Apparently they clean up here periodically."

She socked him in the back. "Not funny."

"I wasn't really spooking you, was I?"

"No." Well, not exactly. Coming across the skeletal remains of someone's long-dead, imprisoned, insane wife—now, *that* would have truly spooked her.

The door opened to reveal a surprisingly brightly lit room. It was wide and round, with an abnormally high ceiling and at least a dozen lead-paned windows recessed into the stone walls. The air was still, warm and musty, and most of the contents of the room were boxed in cardboard or aging wooden trunks. It didn't seem to have antique furniture like the center tower and some of the other upstairs rooms. She supposed nobody would want to carry a dresser or cabinet up that staircase.

"I can't even imagine what's inside all these." She glanced around, feeling like a kid on Christmas morning.

Zach pushed his shoulder gently against hers. "Have at 'er. All this is the property of DFB Incorporated." Then he took the easiest pathway through the boxes to one of the windows, pushing it open and letting in a welcome breeze.

She zeroed in on the trunk that looked the oldest. There, she crouched down on her knees, popped open the center latch, flipped the two end catches and eased up the lid.

Zach squatted beside her. "What did you find?"

"Candleholders." She pushed wads of yellowed newspaper to one side, lifting the first of a matched set of ornate, thickly tarnished silver candleholders. It was heavy in her hand, and Zach took it from her, lifting it and the other, and setting the pair on the floor between them.

"And serving trays," she announced, leaning over the edge of the trunk and digging deeper. To her delight, she also found a tea service and a velvet-lined, mahogany chest of silverware.

"This is great stuff," she enthused, reaching into the depths of the chest.

"Be careful feeling around in there," Zach advised. He reached to the very back of the trunk and pulled out a long, silver object. Rising, he revealed a sheathed sword. He took a step back and withdrew the blade.

Abigail turned, taking the burden off her knees by sitting down. She leaned against the side of the trunk as she gazed up at the sharp, jeweled-hilt sword. It was pretty impressive. Then again, it might be the man brandishing it who was impressive. "That would go great on the restaurant wall."

He stepped back, swishing the blade through the air. "Lord Ashton…" He whistled. "What did you get up to?"

Abigail chuckled. "I hope we find a diary, or some letters or something. I'd love to know more about these people. Hey." She had a sudden idea. "What if we used an old-English-script motif for the menus? We could go with parchment and leather bindings."

"Sure," he agreed, carefully replacing the sword in its sheath. "We'll do them however you want."

She couldn't help feeling pleased by his approval.

He set the sword aside and again peered into the crate. "Here we go."

"What is it?"

"The other sword. It's a matched set. I guess when you challenge someone to a duel, you're obligated to offer evenly matched weapons."

"Or it could be a spare," she reasoned. "Do you think Lord Ashton had a shield to go with them?"

"Not in this trunk." It was obvious they'd come to the paper-lined bottom. "But let's open another."

Nine

Zach watched Abigail's slow smile as, one by one, she unveiled the watercolors they'd discovered behind a canvas sheet against one wall of the north tower. He was content to stand back and observe her reaction to the paintings. Time had slipped away while they worked. Midafternoon, and they were now surrounded by treasures both valuable and absurd. He had no desire and no intention of reminding her that it was getting late.

She favored her left hand as she awkwardly lifted one of the larger paintings. He quickly stepped up and took it away, positioning it so that she could get a better look. It was the view from the cliff beyond Lord Ashton's statue, a man standing in the foreground on a sunny summer day, with Lake Patricia and its two small islands as the backdrop.

"Whoever painted these did a really good job," Abigail observed.

Zach squinted down in front of himself, trying to make out the scrawled signature in the bottom corner. "E. Ashton." At least that's what it looked like to him.

Abigail stepped around the clutter on the floor, dusting off her jeans with one hand as she moved. "E. Ashton," she confirmed.

"Lord Ashton's wife was named Elise."

"I guess she must be the artist. Elise's paintings are *definitely* going on the walls of the restaurant."

"Whatever you say." Zach couldn't keep his gaze from Abigail.

There was a smudge of dust on her smooth cheek. Her eyes were deep gold in the streaming sunshine. Her lips were full and dark, and her mussed hair framed her face like a halo.

"You're beautiful," he breathed.

"Sarcasm?" she returned without missing a beat.

"I'm dead serious." Despite her family's obvious attempts to turn her into some latter-day Cinderella laborer, he'd never met any woman who could hold a candle to her.

"I'm dirty and sweaty, and I haven't worn makeup in two weeks." She held up her blunt, unadorned fingernails. "Look at these."

Setting aside the painting, he reached forward and took her hand, giving in to impulse and gently kissing at her knuckles.

"Doesn't matter," he told her. "They can't erase your beauty."

She fluttered her long lashes. "You're starting to sound like a courtly Lord Ashton."

"I'm beginning to like Lord Ashton."

"I bet he danced a mean quadrille."

Zach lifted her hand and spun Abigail in a pirouette, earning a grin. "He strikes me as more of the pheasant-hunting type. Or maybe wild boar."

"Wild boar?"

"Isn't that what they do in England?"

"I think they go fox hunting. In those tight little red suits. Quite the dandies back then."

"I suppose," he allowed. "I mean, when he wasn't busy loading a cannon or fighting a duel."

"Over the honor of a lady?"

"What other reason would there be to fight a duel?"

"Would you fight for my honor?"

"In a heartbeat." He sobered, his voice going husky, using their joined hands to draw her close.

She didn't pull away, but fear clouded her expression.

"Don't look so scared."

"I'm not scared."

"Good." He couldn't resist brushing a smudge of dust from her cheek.

"Zach?"

"Relax."

"That seems unlikely."

"Let's stop time again."

She went still. "I don't think—"

"I don't mean jump back into bed," he quickly assured her.

"Yes, you do," she countered.

She was right about that, but he wasn't going to press her. "I mean you should stay here. For a couple of days. Help me put together some ideas for the restaurant."

"I told Travis I'd come home today."

"Call him back and tell him you've changed your mind."

"They need me—"

"I know they need you. And I know you love them. And they can have you back. But not yet. Stay here with me and heal." He searched his brain for something else to say, some other argument that might sway her.

He realized that he couldn't bear to let her go back to the ranch while she was still injured. He wanted her here, with him. And, yes, he wanted to sleep with her. He wanted to pull her into his arms and never let her go. But he'd take her with or without lovemaking. He'd take her however he could get her.

She drew a breath. "I don't need to hide to take a few days off. There's some office work at the ranch that I can—"

"Stay, Doll-Face." He gazed deeply into her eyes, all out of reasonable arguments. "Just… Stay."

She was silent for what seemed like an eternity. "Okay," the word whispered out. "For a couple of days."

The tension rushed from his body, and his hand tightened around hers.

He tried to fight the impulse, but he couldn't resist brushing a tender kiss across her soft lips.

The tenderness didn't last. Passion leaped to life inside him, shattering his control. He deepened the kiss, parting her lips, releasing her hand to snake his arm around the small of her back. He reveled in the satisfying feeling of her curves pressed against his taut body. He'd missed her so much, he could barely stand it.

And he wanted more.

He wanted her naked.

He wanted to make love to her so badly that he was nearly shaking with need.

But that wasn't fair. He forced himself to pull back. He let her go, refusing to take advantage of the situation and risk hurting her.

"The west hall," he managed to say.

She blinked at him in obvious confusion, her pupils dilated, lips parted, dark and moist. "Huh?"

He mustered his strength and focused. "We should go look at the west hall. See if it's big enough for the restaurant. I like the high ceilings, and the archways. If it's too small, we could include the mezzanine level. It wraps around the main hall, one story above." Zach knew he was babbling, but it was either that or haul her back into his arms and make love to her on the stone floor, or maybe up against the curved wall, or on one of its long trunks.

Damn it. He had to stop letting his mind wander like that.

"The west hall?" he repeated with a steely will. "We can go down there and take a look." He waited for her response, inordinately proud of his self-control.

She tipped her head to one side, her soft brows going up. "Or," she proposed in a perfectly reasonable tone, "we can stay up here and have sex."

His jaw dropped.

She eased in closer, coming up against him, a sultry smile growing on her face. "Come on, Zach. We both know that's why I'm staying."

"There's more to it than that." There was much more to it than that. Abigail wasn't just about sex to him.

She leaned a cheek against the front of his shirt. "I suppose there's the restaurant. That'll be fun, too."

"Abby," he protested. "I'm not asking you to—"

"I'm just sayin'." She walked her fingertips up his chest. "We can have a quickie now and then concentrate on the restaurant for the rest of the afternoon. Or we can pretend to work, while doing nothing but lusting after each other for the next few hours."

Zach was honestly speechless. The woman was one in a million. No, one in a billion. How many people out there were so forthright and pragmatic? He'd swear she didn't have a manipulative bone in her body.

He put his arms around her and tugged her flush against him. "My room?"

"What's wrong with here?"

"Nothing."

"Good. It'll be more efficient."

"Efficient? That's your priority?"

"A girl gets more done that way."

Chuckling, he popped the snap on her jeans, released the zipper and whisked the denim and her panties down her legs. Then he lifted her and set her on top of a waist-high trunk in one smooth motion.

"Happy to help this girl get things done," he drawled.

She kicked off her boots and got out of her jeans, while he shucked his own pants.

As soon as he was done, she put her hands on his hips and pulled him between her legs. She met his lips in an open-mouthed, carnal kiss that went on and on.

Then she wriggled forward, and their bodies met in intimacy.

"Condom," she prompted.

"Wait a minute, don't you want—"

"What?"

Didn't she want foreplay, soft words, hugs and sexy whispers?

In answer, she braced herself on her elbows, and her legs slipped up to his waist, solidifying the angle between them.

Okay. Apparently not.

"You always this slow on the uptake, Lucky?"

He tore open the condom. "You always this impatient?"

"Never."

"So, it's just me?"

"It's just you."

"Should I be flattered?"

"Absolutely. I'm usually a very deliberate, methodical person."

Taking her at her word, he pressed fully inside.

Her eyes fluttered closed. Her head tipped back, revealing her slender neck. She moaned.

"Good," he agreed, his own voice guttural, mouth going to her neck to taste the delicate skin.

"So good." She arched toward him.

Zach wasted no time. He cupped her bottom with his other hand, pulled her against him, moving immediately into a solid rhythm. Then he stripped off her T-shirt, popped the clasp of her bra and tore off his own shirt, scattering the buttons in his impatience. He needed to feel her hot skin against his, all the length of their bodies.

He inhaled her scent, tasted her sweet lips, cupped her breasts, bringing first one nipple then the other to a beaded point. Her nails dug into his back, her thighs tightened around him. Arousal was like a freight train inside his brain, moving at full speed. There was no stopping it, and there was definitely no turning back.

Abby obviously felt it, too.

He sped up, and she met him thrust for thrust. Her head sank back, and he kissed her neck again, her shoulders, her breasts. His subconscious took over, body arching and withdrawing in a primal rhythm. Her gasps grew higher and shriller, until the contractions of her body sent him completely over the edge.

He locked his knees, stabilizing them both, until the waves of pleasure dissipated. When the strength came back into his muscles, he lifted her, turning her onto his lap, perching himself on the trunk to give his legs a reprieve.

"That wasn't exactly fast," she gasped.

"Complaining?"

"No. But it's a fact, once we get going, we don't seem to want to stop."

He touched his forehead to hers. "I don't ever want to stop."

Her grin was blurry so close to his eyes.

"Maybe long enough to plan a restaurant," she said.

"Maybe long enough for a shower and dinner." Forget the restaurant. They could plan it any old time. Right now, he wanted her in his bed as soon as humanly possible.

"Don't be a slacker, Zach."

A laugh rumbled through him, bringing him partway back to reality. "Nobody's ever accused me of that before."

"It's barely four o'clock. We've got half the day left."

"How late do you usually work?"

"Eight, sometimes nine. It depends."

"You need to join a union or something."

"I'm one of the ranch owners."

"Well, the other ranch owners are taking advantage of you."

"They're working just as hard."

"Most of them left, Abigail."

"You mad at me?"

He drew back in surprise. "No."

"You haven't called me Abigail in a while."

He gazed into her eyes. "I'm not mad at you, Doll-Face. I—" He stopped himself. What the hell had almost popped out of his mouth? "Like you a lot," he finished.

It was true. He liked her. A whole lot. She was so fresh and fun and unpredictable.

"I like you, too, Lucky. But we have a restaurant to plan."

"You'll sleep with me tonight?" he confirmed.

She molded more closely against him. "I'll sleep with you tonight."

His body shuddered in intense relief. He might have missed sleeping with her even more than making love with her. Tonight, she'd lay naked in his arms for hours and hours. Her warm, supple body would wrap around his. He'd sleep deeply, and wake up to her scent, her touch and her voice, knowing she was safe, knowing she was cared for, knowing nothing could harm her as long as he was there.

Abigail knew she was being utterly self-indulgent. She'd been at Craig Mountain for three days now, sleeping with Zach at night, and undertaking what felt like a dream job of planning his restaurant during the day. He was busy with DFB work, either out in the brewery, with the construction contractor, on the phone with Houston or, today, working with Alex who had arrived in person last night.

She'd quickly figured out that Zach was content to leave the restaurant planning entirely in her hands. She dived into the research, contacting other theme restaurants across the country, even recruiting a manager, who'd suggested a head chef. From the west hall today, she was calling graphic design firms and interior decorators, looking for some expertise in putting together themes and branding.

"There you are" came Seth's unexpected voice.

She jolted back in surprise, seeing her brother strolling into the cavernous hall.

"What on earth are you doing here?" she called out.

"I could ask you the same question." His footfalls echoed on the stone floor of the mostly empty room.

She came to her feet, pushing back the big chair. She'd set herself up with a laptop, printer and telephone on what was likely once the master's dining table. It was ornately carved mahogany, with pedestal legs and at least two dozen matching chairs. Right now, it was covered with everything from architectural drawings to fabric swatches and knickknacks from the tower rooms.

"I'm getting better," she answered as Seth made it to her, pulling her into a hug.

"Glad to hear it." He let her go, glancing meaningfully at the cluttered table. "You convalescing or running a business?"

She waved a dismissive hand over the work supplies, swallowing her guilt over focusing on Zach's project instead of her family. "I'm just offering my opinion on a few things."

"Hmm." Seth looked skeptical.

"What's up with you?" she said, changing the topic. "How are things in the mayor's office?" And what was he doing at Craig Mountain?

"Same old, same old," Seth answered, strolling around the table, glancing more closely at her work. "Travis said he'd talked to you yesterday."

"I'll probably head home tomorrow," Abigail found herself saying. "Or maybe the next day."

Seth took in the bandage on her arm. "How's the wound doing?"

"Getting better and better." She moved back to her chair, motioning for Seth to sit in another of the velvet-upholstered dining armchairs.

He took his seat slowly, bracing his hands on the carved, mahogany arms. "So, little sister, what's with this Zach guy?"

She tried to gauge his expression, but he was too good at keeping a poker face. "What do you mean?"

"You want me to be blunt?"

"Please, be blunt." She braced herself.

"Who is he to you? Why are you here instead of at home?"

Abigail gave a studied shrug. "He found me at the side of the highway."

"Travis told me."

"My arm was too sore to drive a stick shift."

"That was three days ago."

"Zach's going to drive me back to the ranch soon." Truth was, it was Abigail herself who was putting off going home. She loved it here. Zach was fun and exhilarating and amazing in bed. She found the restaurant project fulfilling, and she was trying to drag it out just as long as she could.

"I can drive you back today."

"That won't be necess—"

"I'm going out to the ranch anyway."

Abigail couldn't think of a single comeback. There was absolutely no logical reason for her to stay at Craig Mountain instead of going back to the ranch with Seth. She could hardly tell her brother she was having a really great fling. And she sure couldn't tell him she wanted to finish planning the restaurant. It could take weeks, even months. But if she left today with Seth, she wouldn't have a chance to give Zach a proper goodbye, to maybe figure out what happened next.

She hoped something happened next. They'd done their best to stop time once again, to steal a little fantasy with each other amongst their divergent lives. And that might be all that was happening here, a longer, but equally temporary, fling. But she truly hoped it wasn't. She liked Zach. She more than liked Zach. She didn't know what it felt to fall head over heels for somebody, but it had to be close to this.

"Abigail?" Seth prompted.

She blinked at her brother, struggling for the words that would buy her a little more time.

Then Lisa's voice interrupted. She came through the same entry Seth had used. "This place is amazing!" She gaped at the high ceiling. "Did you see the grounds?" she asked Seth. "Hey, Abby. How are you doing? The mayor and I are officially checking out the newest business development in the Lyndon area."

Abigail felt a surge of relief at seeing Lisa. Maybe Lisa could help her finesse the situation. Or at least she could help Abigail stall for a bit.

"You should definitely take a tour of the grounds," Abigail told her brother. "While you're here, check out the new brewery construction. It's moving along at record speed."

"I don't need a tour of the grounds," he responded.

"Well, at least look outside. If you take that staircase—" she pointed to the far end of the rectangular room "—you'll get to the mezzanine above. The bay window down at the other end gives you a view of the lake. But if you look north, you can also see most of the construction."

"Go take a look," Lisa prompted, grasping the back of Seth's chair. "You should at least see the lake and the statue of Lord Ashton."

Seth kept his gaze fixed on Abigail. "Travis doesn't know what to think of this guy."

Abigail met his eyes. "That's because Travis doesn't know him."

"Neither do you."

"I know enough."

"What are you saying?"

"Seth?" Lisa intoned from behind him. "Quit giving your sister the third degree."

"She's needed at the ranch." Seth still spoke directly to Abigail.

"And I'm coming back," she assured him.

"Good." Seth brought his hands down on his thighs.

"Go look out the window," Lisa prompted.

"Fine." Seth came to his feet, tone turning sarcastic. "I don't know why I employ such a bossy woman."

"Because I'm a smart bossy woman." Lisa immediately slipped into the chair Seth had vacated.

He looked down at her. "You're not coming with me?"

"I just saw the statue and the lake."

With a roll of his eyes and a shake of his head, Seth paced for the staircase.

"What the heck is going on?" Lisa asked Abigail, leaning forward on the table. "You're still with one-night-stand guy?"

"I guess it's a five-night stand."

Lisa gave a half laugh, half gasp.

"And what's with Seth?" Abigail returned. "He's acting so…"

"So like *Seth?*"

Abigail supposed that was true. "Does he know anything about Zach?"

"Travis told him Zach tried to get your help with the water license."

"But he thinks I said no, right?"

"He thinks you said no."

"And he doesn't know Zach blackmailed me into it?"

"No, no. Not the blackmail. And not that the two of you had a one-night stand." Lisa grinned. "Well, five-night stand. But he does know about Zach's initial fight with Travis. And he's pretty ticked off about that."

"You can't tell him the rest," Abigail reminded Lisa.

"I'm never going to tell him the rest."

Seth's footfalls sounded directly above them, and they both glanced reflexively up. Abigail leaned closer in and lowered her voice. "Can you help me out here? I'm not ready to go home yet."

Lisa's eyes lit up. "You falling for this guy?"

"Maybe," Abigail admitted, her face growing warm. "Kind of. Just a little bit."

Lisa's grin grew. "He's living in Lyndon now. So you never know what might happen."

Nothing was going to happen, at least nothing that really counted. Not as long as Abigail supported her family, and not as long as Zach wanted her to let them down. "It's all brand-new. And Travis isn't crazy about him. Now Seth doesn't like him."

Lisa waved a dismissive hand. "You can't please your entire family every minute of the day."

"I'm not pleasing anyone at all right now." Every day she stayed here, she was letting Travis down.

"You're pleasing yourself."

"That's not exactly an admirable character trait."

Lisa gave another shrug. "You're human. Live with it."

"I've seen the lake" came Seth's tense voice as he made his way back down the stairs. "And the statue. Are we ready to head home now?"

Abigail's body went stiff. Surely he didn't mean right this second. She was in the middle of working. And Zach didn't even know she was thinking about leaving today.

"Abby needs to say goodbye," Lisa interjected. "Gather her things, thank Zach for his hospitality."

"So this was a social visit?" Seth's jaw was set, his gray eyes hard as steel.

"Come on." Lisa grabbed Abigail's hand, clearly intending to remove her from Seth's line of fire. "Let's go get your stuff."

Abigail allowed herself to be pulled to standing. She glanced longingly from the sketches to the phone messages to the fabric samples. She wasn't ready to leave. She was waiting on return calls. She was waiting on emails, and more samples, and there was still the south tower to explore. But Travis needed her, and Seth was tapping his foot, looking implacable. And she couldn't come up with a single plausible reason to prolong her stay.

Zach entered the west hall, expecting to find Abigail in her usual spot, expertly juggling the hundreds of details around the restaurant project. Instead, he found a grim-looking man in an expensive suit, glaring daggers at him as he approached.

"Can I help you?" Zach asked, searching his brain for context. Was he a building inspector? A tax collector?

"Seth Jacobs," the man announced without offering his hand. "I want you to explain why the hell you've been blackmailing my sister."

Zach stopped short, eyes narrowing. "You're the mayor?"

"I'm the mayor. Now, start talking."

Zach glanced to the corners of the room. "Where's Abigail?"

"None of your business."

"What did she tell you?" Why would Abigail bring Seth in on the secret? What could possibly have happened while Zach was down at the brewery?

"Also none of your business," Seth snapped. "You don't need to worry about how I know. You just need to worry that I do."

"That's all over and done with." Zach's mind was working quickly, trying to assemble pieces of information.

Did Seth know they'd slept together? Did he know Abigail hated working on the ranch? Was everything out in the open? And what did she expect him to do here?

One thing was certain, until he talked to Abby, he wasn't giving her brother any more information.

"*Nothing's* over and done with in my book." Seth took a menacing step forward. "You come after my sister, you deal with me."

Anger flashed deep in the man's eyes. His jaw was set. His fists were clenched. Despite the business suit, he looked a whole lot like his brother, Travis. They might love their sister, but they sure didn't understand her.

Zach responded in the most reasonable tone he could muster. "What's between Abigail and me is none of your business."

"You blackmailed a member of my family. That is my business."

Zach realized Seth was bluffing. The accusation was too vague. "You don't know what happened, do you?"

"If it was sex, you're a dead man. And we mean that literally in Colorado."

"I'm from Texas," Zach responded with equal determination. "If I blackmailed a woman into having sex with me, I'd stand here while you killed me."

Seth drew back in obvious surprise.

Zach used what he hoped was a conciliatory tone. "It might have started off rocky, but things are fine between Abigail and me."

"Well, they're pretty far from fine between me and you."

"She's not doing a single thing she doesn't want to do."

"So says you."

"It's the truth."

"Forgive me if I don't take the word of a blackmailer."

"Former blackmailer."

"You think you're *funny?* Okay, then laugh about this." Seth pointed his index finger to the center of his chest. "I'm the guy who approves your business license. I'm the guy who approves your zoning. And I'm the guy who approves your parking variance."

A block of lead settled itself in Zach's stomach. The idea that Seth could block DFB's move to Lyndon was sickening.

"Not so funny anymore, is it?" Seth taunted.

"You're blackmailing me?"

"Ironic, isn't it?"

"What do you want?"

"I want you to stay away from Abigail. Forever."

"No." The word burst out of Zach. That was the one thing he couldn't do.

"No?" Seth asked with obvious incredulity. "You *want* me to destroy your business?"

"I want you to let your sister make up her own mind." It was all Zach could do to keep silent about Abigail hating the ranch. "Let her make up her mind about me, and about everything else."

"You didn't let her make up her mind about you. You took that choice away from her, didn't you?"

Zach didn't have an answer for that accusation. Seth had him. Zach had behaved shamefully, and there was no arguing the contrary.

"I'm walking out this door. I'm taking Abigail with me. And if you dare touch my sister, talk to my sister, even look at my sister ever again, I will take you and DFB down so fast and so far, you'll never get out of the hole."

"That's abuse of power," Zach pointed out. Seth could lose his office, possibly go to jail.

"That's protecting my family," Seth countered. "And I know a hundred ways to do it and not get caught. Don't test me, Rainer. I'm holding all the cards."

"I'd never hurt her," Zach told him plainly and levelly.

"You already have."

Once again Zach didn't have an answer. Seth was right. He'd already hurt Abigail. He'd betrayed her trust. He'd coerced her. And everything that had happened since was tainted. Seth was right, and Zach was wrong.

Ironic didn't begin to describe the situation.

He gave Seth a curt nod of acquiescence and left the castle. There was no chance Seth would let him say goodbye. Abigail was gone, out of his life, back to her family. He'd never deserved her in the first place.

After two days of silence from Zach, Abigail's guilt turned to frustration. After four days, her frustration turned to anger.

She'd sent him a text. She'd left him a voice mail. So he knew she'd gone home with Seth. But instead of calling to talk about it, he'd cut her off.

She finally realized this was Zach's way of making her choose. And it had worked. She'd take loyalty over betrayal, her family over a one-night stand, any day of the week.

She hoisted a saddle onto Diamond's back, settling it on the hunter-green blanket. She was home, and this was where she was staying.

"Need any help?" her sister Mandy offered from the opposite side of the hitching post as she slipped the bit into Happy-Joe's mouth.

"My arm's fine," Abigail assured her. The gash was nearly healed. She'd have a scar, but hopefully, it would fade over time.

"You always were a trouper."

"That's nothing unique in the Jacobs family."

Mandy grinned in return. She was dressed in blue jeans and a quilted plaid shirt, her favorite Stetson planted firmly on her head. Abigail had slipped into a pair of old blue jeans this morning, topping them with a faded gray T-shirt and a sturdy denim shirt against the cooling autumn air. Her boots were familiar and comfortable, as were the sights, sounds and smells of the ranch.

She inhaled deeply. It was good to be home.

"The Jacksons put their place up for sale," said Mandy.

"I didn't know that." Abigail waited until Diamond exhaled, then swiftly tightened the cinch.

"Prices are down because of the water licenses but Edward's health has been going downhill, and with no kids to take over, they have no choice." Mandy tucked in the end of the cinch strap and adjusted the stirrups.

Abigail felt a twinge of guilt at the mention of the water licenses. Not that she'd done anything that anyone else couldn't have done. Still, she had helped Zach.

She determinedly placed her booted foot in the stirrup and mounted the horse, pushing the man from her mind. Then she gazed around their vast ranchland, the oat fields rippling, the leaves turning. She tugged on her leather gloves and settled the reins across her palm. "I can't imagine selling."

"I'm not worried about the Jacobs clan." Mandy swung up

into her own saddle. "Between the five of us, I'm liking our chances of coming up with a new generation of ranchers. Even Katrina. With Reed's genes mixed in there, we might get a rancher out of her yet."

Abigail laughed at the joke, but her shoulders felt heavy. Between now and the next generation, everybody would be counting on her.

Her cell phone pulsed three short buzzes in her pocket, signaling a text message. Her mind went immediately to Zach, and she stripped off a glove, digging into the front pocket of her jeans while Diamond started into a walk, falling in beside Happy-Joe.

It was Travis, not Zach. Abigail hated the jolt of disappointment. She was going to get past this stupid infatuation. Her family was her future, not Zach. Even if she didn't produce any babies herself, a new generation of Jacobses running around the ranch would be a wonderful thing.

She read the text. "Travis wants us to check on Testa Springs." As the summer ended, watering holes started to run dry, and the cattle needed to be shifted from place to place.

"Makes sense," said Mandy. "We can take the Buttercup Trail."

Abigail replaced her phone and pulled the glove back on, shifting her seat and focusing on the day. "Diesel went up two cents last week."

Though the Jacobs ranch was prosperous, and her father and grandfather's investments provided a cushion against the ups and downs of ranching, Abigail worried about the others in the valley, particularly those with smaller holdings that had higher overhead and big mortgage payments.

"Are you going to tell me about Craig Mountain?" Mandy switched topics.

The question didn't exactly take Abigail by surprise, but that didn't make her any happier about it. Thinking some more about Zach was the last thing she wanted. But she knew being coy with her sister was only going to prolong the conversation.

And there was no reason to hide it from Mandy. Well, most of it anyway.

"Not much to tell," she said breezily, reminded of the times she'd encourage Mandy to go to Caleb's hotel room to be with him. They'd always been honest with each other about men. "I met a guy. Hurt my arm. We had a fling. And I'm now home again."

Mandy turned to look at her, obviously fighting a grin. "I hate it when you go into so much detail."

"That's all there was to it."

"It's going to be a long ride."

"I know how long the ride is."

"I'm just saying you might want to help the time pass by filling in a few more details."

"They're building a restaurant up at the brewery," Abigail offered.

"I'm more interested in what Zach—it's Zach, right?—in what Zach looks like naked."

"Does your husband know you're wondering about that?"

Mandy laughed. "Was he great? I mean, he must have been great. You stayed up there five days."

And she would have stayed longer if not for Seth. And she'd go back, if not for Zach's stubborn insistence she walk away from her family.

"It was great," she admitted to Mandy. "He's a smart, fun, sexy guy, and he was letting me help him design his restaurant. I liked that," she admitted.

"Why'd you leave?"

"Irreconcilable differences."

"What, over the tablecloths and menu choices?"

"Something like that."

"Abby."

"Can we drop it?" Abigail's tone was sharper than she'd intended.

Mandy went silent. Abigail focused on the sound of the horses breathing and their hooves rustling the grass as they made their way up a slight rise.

Mandy's tone went sympathetic. "Did he break your heart, Abby?"

Abigail's chest tightened, and her throat tingled in reaction. She wanted to be strong, keep the secret to herself. But she needed her sister's shoulder to lean on. "Only a little bit."

They came to the top of the rise, and a vast valley spread out in front of them. Abigail stopped Diamond to take a long look.

"His fault or yours?" Mandy asked softly.

"His. Mostly. Well, mine, too." She had left abruptly with Seth. Maybe she should have told her brother to mind his own business. Maybe she should have stood up to him in that moment and bought herself a few more days with Zach.

"So what are you going to do about it?" Mandy asked.

Abigail shook her head in answer, both to her sister and to herself. "There's nothing I can do."

"You can talk to him. These things never run smoothly. Heaven knows Caleb and I had our share of rocky moments."

"Zach's not Caleb."

"You can still talk to him."

Abigail gripped the saddle horn. There was a catch she couldn't quite keep out of her voice. "I've left messages. He didn't call back."

Without giving Mandy a chance to respond, she kicked Diamond into a trot.

Abigail couldn't seem to get Mandy's words out of her head. Was it better to try to talk to Zach or would a smart woman simply walk away? She couldn't decide. And she was afraid her judgment was clouded by her intense desire to see him again, no matter what the circumstance.

Then again, she reasoned, if her own judgment was clouded, maybe she should go with Mandy's. Mandy was a smart woman. Her advice had been specific and concrete. Abigail should take it. After five miserable days she didn't see how things could get worse.

She knew she could use Ozzy as an excuse to return to Craig Mountain. When she'd left with Seth and Lisa, she hadn't been able to find the puppy. Not surprising, since Ozzy had taken such a shine to Zach. They'd probably been together.

Mind finally made up, she headed for the brewery, easily finding Zach alone in an office.

She breezed in, playing it cool, pretending there hadn't been a seismic shift in their relationship. Half of her hoped he'd pull her into his arms. The other half knew that was a hopeless fantasy.

"I tried to call you," she began, hoping against hope for a simple, logical explanation that would switch everything back to normal.

But instead of answering, he stepped behind the wide desk, obviously putting some distance between them. His expression was guarded. "You shouldn't have come here, Abigail."

Her faint hope fled. "You should have returned my call."

"I didn't want to disturb you. I knew you'd be busy. You've told me what it's like on the ranch." His tone was cool. His eyes were cold.

She wanted to run from the chill, but she forced herself to step closer, coming up against the desk. She gathered her courage. "Is this you pouting?"

"No."

"I didn't pick my family over you."

"I didn't say you did."

"Then why won't you talk to me?"

"We're talking now."

"This isn't talking."

He drew a tight breath. "Trust me, Doll-Face. This is *talking*. And you need to listen." His words dropped like icicles. "It was always going to be temporary between us."

Her lungs went tight, and she couldn't catch her breath.

"And it's over," he finished, and her heart sank like a stone.

She shouldn't have come. She'd completely misjudged the situation. How she wished she'd stayed away. He'd wanted her to leave.

She swallowed hard, a sick feeling bubbling up from the pit

of her stomach. Oh, no. Had he been *waiting* for her to leave? Maybe he'd asked her to stay only out of politeness.

She took a shaky step backward, a chill coming over her body, while humiliation washed through her. The fling had run its course, and she'd embarrassed them both by showing up like this.

She struggled to speak, her voice going small. "I came back to get Ozzy."

Something flashed through Zach's eyes. "Ozzy's fine."

She gathered her pride. "I'm sure you took good care of him, and I thank you for that."

"He can stay."

A fresh flash of pain seared Abigail's chest.

"I don't think he likes the ranch," said Zach.

"He'll get used to the ranch." The puppy was hers, not Zach's.

"Why should he have to do that?"

"Because it's his home. He's my dog, not yours." If she couldn't have Zach, she could at least have Ozzy. She knew her emotions were off kilter, but giving up the puppy suddenly seemed like a final defeat.

"Leave him here, Abby."

Her voice rose. "I want my dog."

"He's more my dog than yours."

"That's not true."

Zach braced his hand on the desktop. "He's happy here. Let him be happy. Why don't you want him to be happy?"

"I do want him to be happy. I want him to be happy with me."

"You Jacobses are all alike," Zach snapped.

"What is that supposed to mean?" He'd barely met any other Jacobses.

"It means…" Zach paused, and for a split second she saw raw pain in his dark eyes. He backed away from her. "It means…"

"Zach?"

His back came flush against the office wall. "You need to leave. Right now."

Her anger immediately vanished, replaced by a hollow loneliness that shattered the last vestiges of her pride. "What did I miss? What happened?"

"Life happened. Your life. My life." He crossed his arms over his chest, and his stare went cold again. "Time started up again, Abby."

Her heart ached, and her stomach clenched. "So you're ending it between us."

"Yes."

"It was a fling, and you're ending it."

"How many ways do I have to say it?"

She tried to laugh, but it didn't quite come off. "I'm sorry. I guess I'm a bit slow on the uptake. I've never done anything like this before."

She'd never had a one-night stand, never had a fling, never fallen in love and had her heart broken.

"I'm sorry," she said again, voice breaking.

"It's all right," Zach returned, without a trace of emotion.

"You can keep Ozzy." Everything Zach had said was true. Ozzy was happier at Craig Mountain. He and Zach should stay together.

"You can take him," Zach unexpectedly offered.

But Abigail shook her head, backing toward the door. She might as well make a clean break of it. She didn't know what she'd expected by coming out here. But she hadn't come after Ozzy. She'd come after Zach.

Zach didn't want her. It had only ever been about sex for him. Well, sex and the water license. And maybe it had only been about the water license. The sex was a bonus. He really was lucky. He got everything he wanted and then some.

She groped for the doorknob, twisting it with a slick palm, letting herself out and rushing back down the hallway, desperate to end this sorry episode of her life.

Ten

Zach was going through his days on autopilot. Though he was far from being an expert, he strongly suspected he'd fallen in love with Abigail. Worse than missing her was the knowledge that he'd hurt her, and he was now powerless to do anything about it. He had to fight with himself every single day to keep from calling to see how she was feeling.

One day he spotted her on Main Street. He nearly called out, but then he saw Travis coming out of the hardware store behind her. He was under no illusion that Travis felt any differently than his brother, Seth. Zach gripped the door handle of his Jaguar, watching her move alongside the ranch pickup truck, wondering if she'd recognize him from this distance, honestly not sure what he would do if she saw him. He didn't think he could bring himself to ignore her.

She was carrying a cardboard box. It was impossible to tell if it was heavy, but the urge to stride down the block and lift it from her arms was overpowering. And then he saw she was limping. He swore from between clenched teeth.

What had happened this time? Had a cow stepped on her foot? Or maybe she'd tripped and twisted an ankle, or come off a horse again, or maybe she'd fallen off a roof. Angry at her, angry at her family, and furious with himself at having abandoned her, he yanked open the driver's door. He slammed his way into the car and peeled out of town.

He brooded in the depths of the castle until Alex caught up with him in his suite that night.

"Missed you at the meeting this afternoon," Alex said easily, but his expression was watchful as he crossed the room, taking a spot on the sofa.

"Got busy," Zach responded vaguely, not wanting to talk about his abrupt departure from Lyndon. He rose and made his way to the makeshift bar to pour them each a scotch.

"No big deal," said Alex, letting it go. "Accounting wants a new software package. Ariel-something. They say it'll pay for itself in staff savings within the next couple of years."

Zach collected the drinks and turned back. "Did you okay it?"

"Wanted to run it by you first."

Zach walked over to Alex and handed him his drink. "Whatever you think."

"I think yes."

"Good enough." Zach sat himself down.

Ozzy immediately waddled over, dropped onto his rear end and whimpered at Zach's feet. Zach automatically scooped the puppy up into his lap.

"Laziest dog in the world," Alex mused.

"He's not lazy."

"He can't even be bothered to jump into your lap."

"He's not lazy. Give the little guy a break."

Alex chuckled.

Annoyed, Zach stared levelly at his friend. "They were going to put him down. Because he's imperfect, and nobody wanted him. You know what that's like."

Alex took a sip of his scotch. "I do know what that's like. But I don't think he should use it as a crutch for the rest of his life."

"One of his legs is shorter than the other," Zach felt compelled to explain. "And he's blind in one eye. It's hard for him to jump."

"He'll never learn if you don't make him try."

"He is trying," said Zach, anger percolating inside him. "I can tell he's trying. But he's not cut out for jumping. He's not cut out to be some robust ranch hand, running after cattle and horses."

"Ranch hand?"

"He'll get hurt." The day's frustrations clouded Zach's brain, coalescing into outright anger. "He might even get killed. And the people who claim to love her should stop putting her in danger."

Alex peered over the rim of his glass. "Her?"

"Huh?"

"You said her."

Zach gave himself a shake. "I meant him."

"You said her."

Zach downed his drink in one swallow. "He's just a little puppy. I'm going to take care of him. So sue me."

Alex rocked back. "Okay, Zach. What the hell's going on?"

"Nothing."

"You're all bottled up."

"I've been working hard, and I'm tired. We're all tired."

"Bull," said Alex. "You love this stuff. When things get frantic and risky, you love it even more."

"I hate it." Zach hated everything today. He hated uprooting their headquarters. He hated moving halfway across the country. And he especially hated depending on Seth Jacobs. If he didn't need to set DFB up in Lyndon, nobody, *nobody* would stop him from going to Abigail.

Alex was silent for a long minute. He polished off his own drink. "It's her, isn't it?"

Zach tried to take another drink, but his glass was empty, nothing but a sip of melted ice on the bottom. "I don't know what you're talking about."

"You've been on edge since Abigail left."

Zach gave a grunt of disagreement.

"Why don't you call her?"

Zach would like nothing better than to call her. "Not gonna happen."

"I know what you're going through. I've been there with Stephanie. You're going to feel like this until you call her."

"I can't call her."

"I know you *think* you can't call her. But, believe me, you can. You'll get used to the indignity that comes with having a girlfriend."

"You think this is about my dignity?" Zach scoffed. If it had been that simple, he'd have kept her here when she came back for Ozzy. No, that wasn't true. If it had been as simple as his dignity, he'd have never let her leave in the first place.

"What else would it be about?" Alex asked.

Zach wasn't a heart-to-heart kind of guy, but he was too tired to fight it tonight, too tired to do anything but admit the truth.

"It's about you," he admitted to Alex. "You and DFB and everybody else. If it was just about me, I'd do whatever it took. In a heartbeat. Anything."

"You're in love with her," Alex stated.

"Absolutely." There wasn't a doubt in Zach's mind.

Alex rose, crossed the floor and retrieved the scotch bottle. He poured a measure into each glass. "Then it's not about me."

Zach contemplated the new drink, a sense of eerie calm coming over him as his mind went places he never could have imagined. "How would you feel about starting over?" he asked softly.

Alex sat back down. "Starting over how?"

"You and me, in a cheap basement suite, working as bartenders again while we save up a down payment for another business."

"Not great," said Alex. "But I'd do it. Why?"

Zach hesitated a moment longer. "Because her brother threatened me."

Alex was clearly confused. "Threatened you with what?"

Zach set the glass down. "The mayor told me that if I ever so much as spoke to his sister again, he'd turn down our business license and make it impossible for DFB to operate in Lyndon."

"Why?"

"He thinks he's protecting Abigail. He knows I blackmailed her. I imagine he thinks I coerced her into sleeping with me."

Alex stared reflexively into space, and the minutes ticked by.

Zach knew he'd put his friend in an impossible position. He was sorry about that. But he didn't think he could bring himself to abandon Abigail.

When Alex finally spoke, there was a thread of laughter in his voice. "He actually forced you to choose between her and me?"

"He did."

"And you chose me? I'm flattered, Zach. But…you're an idiot."

"Choosing her would have destroyed the company."

"You're still an idiot."

"Are you saying I should have turned him down?" Zach challenged.

"I'm saying, for starters, you should have told me we were being blackmailed."

"Yeah," Zach was forced to agree. "I should have told you that."

How many other mistakes had he made in all this? He found himself picturing Abigail in his robe, the night he'd rescued her from the highway, her bandaged arm, the fading bruises, her sore rib cage. His stomach churned.

"I can't leave her there, Alex. It's not right. She's not happy. The work's dangerous. I'm afraid it might kill her."

"So go get her."

"I do, and I risk everything we've ever worked for."

"We'll build something else." Alex made it sound ridiculously simple.

"And what about our employees?"

"If worse comes to worst, we'll sell the assets and give them all a fat severance package."

Zach snapped his fingers. "Just like that?"

"You don't get to give up Abigail for me, Zach. Because if

I find the right woman, and I have to choose—" Alex grinned and shrugged "—you're toast, buddy."

"Good to know where I stand."

"Isn't it?"

It was.

And it was great to know that Alex had his back, just as he always had. No brother in the world could be more loyal than Alex. Because of him, Zach didn't need to stand around and watch Abigail suffer. He could do something about it, damn the consequences.

When Abigail heard Zach's voice in the foyer of the ranch house, she shot to her feet from the sofa, gaping in astonishment as he elbowed his way past Travis, wheeling into the living room.

Her brother Seth jumped up from an armchair, squaring his shoulders and widening his stance. "What the hell are you doing here?"

Lisa appeared from the kitchen, obviously drawn by the raised voices. She stopped in the archway and took in the three men.

"Zach?" Abigail managed to say, the breath leaving her body. What had happened? Why did he look so angry?

Instead of responding to her, he spoke to Seth. "You," he growled, "can take your business license and shove it."

Travis stopped short behind Zach.

"Zach?" Abigail repeated, taking a step forward, half hopeful, half confused.

"Get out of this house," Seth ordered.

"I will close my business," Zach vowed, his voice low and menacing.

"What the hell?" Travis interjected.

"Leave," Seth repeated.

Zach didn't take his gaze off Seth. "I'll chuck it all and start from scratch before I sacrifice Abby."

Sacrifice her?

"Have you lost your mind?" Travis demanded of Zach.

Good question.

"I'll do whatever she wants. I'll hire her," said Zach, still fixating on Seth. "I'll marry her. I'll protect her. The one thing I won't do is let the family who supposedly loves her work her into the ground."

"That's enough," Seth shouted.

"What's he talking about?" Travis had also turned his attention to his brother.

"Nothing," said Seth.

Zach gave a cold laugh. He turned to Travis. "Your brother didn't tell you he was blackmailing me?"

Abigail gaped at Seth.

His nostrils were flared, and his face had turned ruddy.

"Seth?" Travis insisted.

"He's the one who was blackmailing her."

Abigail's stomach dropped like a stone. Her gaze shot to Lisa, but Lisa shook her head in incomprehension.

"He seduced her," Seth continued. "Then he threatened to run to us with the tale."

Zach coughed out a sharp laugh. "You think *that* was my threat? That I'd kiss and tell?"

"Stop it!" Abigail demanded, afraid she knew where Zach was going.

"I threatened—"

"Shut up, Zach."

Zach stared coolly into her eyes but kept right on speaking. "To tell you that she hates working at the ranch."

The room went completely silent.

Abigail mouthed the word no, slowly shaking her head in denial.

"They need to know, Abby."

No, they didn't. They never needed to know. She couldn't believe Zach had betrayed her. "You promised," she whispered.

"I guess I lied."

"How could you?"

Travis stepped up, clamping a hand on Zach's shoulder. "Time for you to leave."

"We need to talk," Zach said to Abigail.

"Why did you come back?"

His tone went soft, and so did his brown eyes. "Because I couldn't stay away."

"Out," said Travis.

But Lisa spoke up, advancing on Seth. "What did you do?"

Seth puffed out his chest. "I protected my sister."

Abigail stood in mute misery, knowing she'd been the cause of all this.

Zach's voice was deliberate. "Mayor Jacobs advised me that if I ever spoke to his sister again, he'd deny the DFB business license and bankrupt my company."

"*He* was blackmailing *her,*" Seth protested.

"How did you know that?" asked Lisa.

"Stop it!" Abigail cried. "Everyone, please, just stop." She couldn't stand that Seth had compromised his principles. And she hated that Zach had outed her.

Lisa's arm closed on her shoulders.

Abigail found herself searching Zach's face, as if his expression might give her a hint of why he was doing this.

"You hate the ranch?" Travis asked.

"She's had enough," said Lisa.

Zach shook off Travis's hand, turning on him. "You might want to think about letting her leave this place before you kill her."

Travis sneered. "Don't be absurd."

"Ask her for an inventory of her bruises someday."

Seth had gone quiet. Now he turned a concerned look on Abigail.

"Get out," Travis ordered.

"Right," Zach capitulated. "I'm leaving." Then his icy stare took in both brothers. "But that doesn't mean I'm gone."

His last look was for Abigail. His eyes turned to mocha, and his mouth flexed in a half smile. His deep tone brought back a thousand memories. "Take your time, Doll-Face. Decide what you want to do and let me know."

* * *

An hour later, Abigail blinked against the shaft of light from the hallway as her sister Mandy pushed open the door and stepped into the dim bedroom, quietly pulling it shut behind her.

Abigail shifted into a sitting position on the bed, drawing up her knees. "It didn't take them long to send for reinforcements."

Mandy smiled as she padded across the room, wrapping her hand around the newel post on the footboard. "Sounds like I missed all the fun."

"You call that fun?"

"I call it exciting." Mandy sat down at the foot of the big bed and leaned back.

"It was that," Abigail allowed.

"Your life's not usually that exciting."

"Not so you'd notice." Though, lately, it had had its moments.

"So, what's the real story with this guy?"

"It's a bit complicated."

Her sister shrugged. "I'm not going anywhere." Then she grinned. "Seriously, Abby. I'm not going anywhere anytime soon. So you might as well start talking."

"I met him in Lyndon." Abigail settled back against the headboard, preparing to give her sister the whole story. Though she felt battered and bruised, and confused by Zach's behavior, she felt strangely calm. It was all out in the open now. For better or worse, they could all stop sneaking around.

"When?" Mandy prompted into the silence.

"Election night. He was a stranger then, probably the only guy in town who didn't know who I was. He thought I was elegant and sophisticated."

"You are elegant and sophisticated."

Abigail's glance went to her tattered fingernails. "Not usually."

"You were that night. It was one great dress."

"It was," Abigail agreed. She thought back to her and Zach's nighttime picnic. "I was pretty hot that night. It was all very sexy. I wouldn't let him tell me his name, and I refused to tell him mine. But we slept together."

"No way."

"Way. It was great. And then I sneaked away the next morning."

"And he tracked you down to blackmail you?"

"No. He didn't know who I was." Abigail believed that now. "He needed a variance on his water license. Somebody gave him my name. And when I refused to help him, that's when he blackmailed me."

"And you're still sleeping with him."

"Yes. Well, I was until Seth threatened him, and he broke it off." At least Abigail now understood Zach's sudden withdrawal. She was going to have a long talk with both her brothers.

"He's a great guy," Abigail continued. "In a ridiculous situation." She thought back to the DFB employees she'd met in Houston, and his determination to do right by them. And when you added to that Seth's blackmail, and Zach's stunning reaction tonight… A reaction that was only now coming clear inside her head.

She sat up straighter. "I'm pretty sure he said something about marrying me down there."

"I heard. Lisa told me."

"What do you think he meant by that?" Could it have been metaphorical? Even if she took into account Zach's rather single-minded determination to get her away from the ranch, offering to marry her seemed a bit extreme.

"Let's see…" Mandy tapped her temple with her index finger. "What could a man possibly mean when he offers to marry a woman?" She gave an elongated pause. "I know. Maybe he wants to *marry* you."

"Why?"

"To love, honor and keep you all the days of his life?"

"That's silly. Zach doesn't love me."

"You sure about that?"

Abigail wasn't sure about anything right now. And her head was starting to ache.

She changed the subject. "What on earth was Seth thinking?"

"That he was protecting you."

"Ha, he botched that. I'm a grown woman. He needs to stop interfering in my life. So does Travis."

Mandy leaned forward as if to share a secret. "Maybe if you hadn't lied to him, lied to all of us."

"I never lied."

"You didn't tell us you hated the ranch."

"I don't hate the ranch."

"You hate working on the ranch."

Abigail pushed back her messy hair. A sheen of sweat had formed at the hairline. "Yeah," she admitted. "I hate working on the ranch."

"You should have said something."

"And then what? Leave Travis stuck here all alone?"

"He can hire more help."

Abigail's voice rose. "It's not the same. You know it's not the same."

Mandy scooted to the middle of the bed, placing a hand on Abigail's upraised knee. "That doesn't mean you get to be the sacrificial lamb. Travis doesn't want you to do that. None of us want you to do that. Would you want Katrina to do that?"

"It's different with Katrina."

"It's not different at all." Mandy squared her shoulders. "You're not staying, Abby. We're not going to let you stay."

Abigail gave a sad smile. She had mixed emotions about that. She didn't want to abandon Travis, but she desperately wanted her freedom.

Mandy wasn't finished. "And while you're thinking about where to go, did you happen to give a listen to what Zach said down there? Did you watch him stand up to Seth and Travis? Did you see that he was willing to give up everything for you? His company. His fortune. Alex, and everything they've ever worked for. And he didn't know how our brothers would react. There were two of them and only one of him, and he barged onto their land to get you."

Abigail had seen all that. She'd been shell-shocked at the time. But Mandy was right—it was pretty amazing.

"Love doesn't get much better than that," said Mandy.

Abigail's chest squeezed tight. Could it be true? They pushed and pulled and prodded each other. He was frustrating and opinionated, and she was stubborn. But they also made amazing love. And they laid for hours in each other's arms afterward. And they shared joys and fears and secrets. And if she'd had her way, she might never have left Craig Mountain.

She loved Zach. She loved him so very much.

Mandy tossed back her hair. "So, what are you going to do now?"

"I don't know."

"Yes, you do."

Abigail groaned at the bedroom ceiling. "I should never have let him walk out of here."

"You love him."

"Yes."

"Then you should have thrown yourself in his arms, told him that and walked away from the ranch with him by your side."

"I'd be halfway to Craig Mountain by now." Abigail paused, hope glowing to life inside her. "Is it possible that he really wants to marry me?"

"He asked you."

"In a roundabout way."

"In a very public and possibly hazardous way. He didn't know how Seth and Travis would react."

Abigail's heart thudded, and the hope grew stronger.

"Go ask him," Mandy whispered. "Better yet, answer him. Tell him you love him. Say yes to the marriage proposal."

"Drive on up to Craig Mountain." Abigail couldn't help remembering what had happened last time she'd tried that.

"Yes."

"Tell him I love him."

"Yes."

"Step off an emotional cliff with no safety net."

"He already did that for you."

Abigail felt herself smile.

He had. He'd waltzed right in here and gambled everything. Mandy was right—the very least Abigail could do was meet him halfway.

She put her hand on top of Mandy's and squeezed. "I'm going to Craig Mountain."

"You want me to drive?"

"I think I need to do this alone."

"It's late. And it's a long way. Caleb will—"

"I'm a big girl, Mandy. I can drive myself."

Mandy sucked a breath through her teeth. "Yes, you can. Call me when you get there."

Abigail came to her feet, feeling an overwhelming urge to run to the nearest vehicle and speed to the highway. "I might be busy." She started for the door.

"Then phone me after," Mandy called out. "And drive carefully."

On the stone front patio of the castle, Zach lounged in a deep, wood-slat chair, Alex in the one next to him, Ozzy curled at his feet, a bottle of cold C Mountain Ale condensing against his left palm.

"So, you proposed," Alex was saying. "But you left without getting an answer."

"She was pretty upset by the whole thing," Zach responded. "I don't think she's had time to think it through."

Ugly as it was, he didn't regret his actions tonight. He'd meant every word he said to Seth and Travis, and to Abigail. Whatever she wanted, whatever she needed, he was here, and he wasn't going anywhere.

"You probably should have waited for an answer," said Alex.

"Maybe," Zach admitted. He'd gone over it a thousand times on the drive back. But he truly didn't know if he should have stayed. "Maybe I should have kidnapped her when I had the chance."

Alex chuckled. "I can't see her brothers letting you haul her out of the family house."

"I suppose."

They both took a swig of beer, while the crisp wind whistled across the lake, crackling the bright fall leaves and sending them fluttering down to the grass around the castle.

"So we might be bankrupt, and we might not," Alex mused.

"I don't think Seth will hold it against us."

By the end there, it was obvious Seth was rethinking the situation. Out of everyone in that room, Zach was willing to bet Seth got that Zach would defend Abigail against anyone, including her family.

Alex contemplated his beer bottle. "Which means, the company is saved, and we'll still be able to drink free of charge?"

"Damn fine beer," Zach intoned, chuckling at the memory of their silly, teenage name for the company. Their original plan had been to buy a small brewery, create jobs for themselves and be able to drink for free. That's as far as their dreams had gone in the early days.

"DFB," Alex echoed. "It's been one amazing trip, buddy."

A pair of headlights appeared in the distance, flashing through the trees as the vehicle bounced on the rough road. It was coming in at quite a clip.

"You don't suppose…" Alex ventured.

"A guy can hope." Zach's chest tightened. He took a reflexive swig from the bottle, draining it and setting it on the patio beside his chair.

Restless, he came to his feet, gazing into the night, waiting for the moment when the vehicle came around the bend and he'd know if it was her or not.

"Jacobs Cattle Company." Alex spoke in the same moment Zach read the logo on the door of the blue truck.

"I hope it's not Travis with a shotgun." Zach squinted at the windshield, but the parking-lot lights were reflecting off the glass, and he couldn't see inside.

"I thought you said he wouldn't hold it against you."

"That was Seth."

Travis was definitely a wild card with an attitude.

The truck rocked to a halt.

It was her.

Zach's chest tightened further as she slammed her way out of the driver's seat. She rounded the hood, wearing scruffy jeans, a gray T-shirt and tan cowboy boots. Her hair was mussed, her makeup nonexistent, and her mouth was pursed in a moue of determination.

God, she was beautiful.

"Yes," she shouted shortly as she mounted the stairs.

"Yes, what?" he called back.

She trotted toward him. "You told me to decide what I wanted."

"I did."

She stopped in front of him. "And to let you know."

She didn't look angry, and he dared to really hope.

"Uh-huh," he prompted, gazing into those gorgeous golden eyes.

He was vaguely aware of Alex coming to his feet behind him.

"Hi, Alex," said Abigail, her glance flicking past Zach's shoulder.

Zach touched an index finger to the bottom of her chin, turning her attention back to him. "Yes, what?"

A beat went by. "Yes, I'll marry you."

Pure, unadulterated joy shot through him, but he kept it together. "You will?"

A trace of uncertainty crossed her face. It was adorable. "Were you serious? Or were you just trying to protect me?"

He had to struggle to keep a straight face. He also had to struggle to keep from hauling her into his arms and kissing the life out of her.

"I was trying to protect you," he admitted. He tried to pause, but he was impatient. "I was also trying to love you."

"Gettin' anywhere with that?" she asked, her spunk clearly back.

"Yeah." He gave in and wrapped his arms around her waist. "I've succeeded. Completely."

"Then say it."

"I love you."

"Good."

"Your turn."

"I love you, too, Lucky. A whole lot." She came up on her toes, snaking her arms around his neck.

He met her halfway in a searing kiss.

"Uh, Zach?" came Alex's voice.

Zach broke the kiss and turned. "Are you still here?"

Abigail giggled against his chest.

"I thought you might want this." Alex tossed a small wooden box that Zach caught in midair. "I found it in the north tower."

Puzzled, Zach flipped the brass catch with his thumb and opened the top. There sat a gorgeous little emerald-and-diamond ring, the brilliant stones nestled in polished gold.

"I don't know its history," said Alex. "But then, we orphans never really know for sure, do we?"

"We never do," Zach agreed. An heirloom ring from Craig Mountain Castle. Somehow, it seemed fitting.

"And now I'm leaving." Alex's footsteps sounded on the porch until the door closed behind him.

Zach turned to show Abigail the ring.

"Will you marry me?" he whispered. "I love you so much."

"Yes," she breathed, her eyes sparkling brighter than the ring. Then she looked down. "It's absolutely gorgeous. Lord Ashton's?"

"I'm really starting to like that guy."

The first day of spring was opening night at Lord Ashton's Alehouse. Over the months Abigail had worked on the project, the restaurant had expanded until it was a whole lot larger than Zach had first envisioned. There'd been a buzz about the place around the whole state since New Year's, and the restaurant was booked up past the end of the month.

A bright wood fire roared in the massive fireplace, vintage black tools hanging from hooks against the worn stones. Lord Ashton's swords and shields decorated the walls, and Abigail had even found a couple of suits of armor to place in the corners of the room.

The dinning tables were made of worn, rough-hewn beams. An elaborate candelabrum sat in the center of each one. The chairs were upholstered in soft leather, designed to look worn, with the wooden arms and backs crafted to look antique. Lady Elise Ashton's paintings graced the entrance, and the multitude of sunken windows were decorated with heavy, emerald velvet curtains.

"Is it really wild boar?" Mandy asked, pointing at the leather-bound menu from her place at the table next to Abigail.

"They assure me it is," Abigail answered, smiling around the big table at Seth and Travis, Mandy and her husband, Caleb. Alex was at the foot of the table kitty-corner to Lisa. And even Reed and Katrina had flown in from New York City for the weekend. Her parents were still in Denver, settling in nicely to the social life in a retirement complex.

"I'm going for it," said Mandy. "And I'm definitely trying the Yorkshire pudding."

"I don't know how you people can eat so much," Katrina put in from across the table.

"Try the garden salad," Abigail advised her youngest sister. The downside to being a famous ballerina was keeping your figure so trim.

"I'll be eating even more pretty soon," said Mandy.

"Going on a trail ride?" asked Seth, helping himself to one of the fresh rolls placed in baskets in the middle of the table.

"Eating for two," Mandy announced matter-of-factly.

The wide, proud grin that stretched across Caleb's face confirmed the news.

Abigail squealed. "You're pregnant!"

Mandy nodded, while Abigail pulled her into a tight hug.

The men offered congratulations to Caleb, and Katrina rushed around the table to join her sisters.

"I'm going to be an auntie," Abigail breathed.

"I can't wait to take her to plays and shops and museums," said Katrina.

"Might be a boy." Mandy laughed.

Katrina pooh-poohed with a wave of her hand. "If it is, you can always try again."

Abigail laughed, glancing down at her sister's flat stomach. "Do Mom and Dad know?"

"I called them this morning."

While her brothers came around to hug Mandy, Abigail felt Zach's hand wrap around hers. He urged her to him, out of the fray, then drew her down onto his lap in the roomy armchair at the head of the table.

"What about you?" he whispered in her ear.

"What about me?" she whispered back.

"You interested in having kids?"

"I am." She rested her cheek against his, inhaling his familiar scent and letting her body mold against his strength, while her family's voices seemed to fade. "You?"

"I'm the only one of my line," he said, voice gruff. "So, yeah. I'd like to carry it on."

Abigail's heart squeezed hard.

"We can have lots of children," she told him around a suddenly clogged throat. "You, Zach Rainer, are going to be the start of something big."

"Can we start now?"

She couldn't help smiling at that. "We haven't even had the appetizer yet."

"I don't need food. I need you."

"After dessert," she whispered with a surreptitious glance over her shoulder to the commotion around Mandy. "We'll go get pregnant."

He stared deeply, lovingly into her eyes. "Do you think we should get married first?"

"Sure."

He hesitated. "So, we'll wait?"

"I'm thinking, if we take the Jaguar, we can be over the Nevada border in six hours."

He drew back. "Elope?"

She nodded.

"Won't that upset your family?"

She smoothed a hand across his cheeks, burrowing her fingers in his hair and moving in close. "I've stopped living for my family, Lucky." She kissed him gently on the lips. "I'm living for you now. And we should do whatever we want."

"Oh, Doll-Face," he groaned, hugging her tight. "Marry me. Do it now."

* * * * *

PASSION

Harlequin *Desire*

COMING NEXT MONTH
AVAILABLE JUNE 12, 2012

#2161 HIS MARRIAGE TO REMEMBER
The Good, the Bad and the Texan
Kathie DeNosky

#2162 A VERY PRIVATE MERGER
Dynasties: The Kincaids
Day Leclaire

#2163 THE PATERNITY PROMISE
Billionaires and Babies
Merline Lovelace

#2164 IMPOSSIBLE TO RESIST
The Men of Wolff Mountain
Janice Maynard

#2165 THE SHEIKH'S REDEMPTION
Desert Knights
Olivia Gates

#2166 A TANGLED AFFAIR
The Pearl House
Fiona Brand

REQUEST YOUR FREE BOOKS!
2 FREE NOVELS PLUS 2 FREE GIFTS!

♦ Harlequin®

Desire

ALWAYS POWERFUL, PASSIONATE AND PROVOCATIVE

YES! Please send me 2 FREE Harlequin Desire® novels and my 2 FREE gifts (gifts are worth about $10). After receiving them, if I don't wish to receive any more books, I can return the shipping statement marked "cancel." If I don't cancel, I will receive 6 brand-new novels every month and be billed just $4.30 per book in the U.S. or $4.99 per book in Canada. That's a saving of at least 14% off the cover price! It's quite a bargain! Shipping and handling is just 50¢ per book in the U.S. and 75¢ per book in Canada.* I understand that accepting the 2 free books and gifts places me under no obligation to buy anything. I can always return a shipment and cancel at any time. Even if I never buy another book, the two free books and gifts are mine to keep forever.

225/326 HDN FEF3

Name _____ (PLEASE PRINT) _____

Address _____ Apt. # _____

City _____ State/Prov. _____ Zip/Postal Code _____

Signature (if under 18, a parent or guardian must sign)

Mail to the **Reader Service:**

IN U.S.A.: P.O. Box 1867, Buffalo, NY 14240-1867
IN CANADA: P.O. Box 609, Fort Erie, Ontario L2A 5X3

Not valid for current subscribers to Harlequin Desire books.

Want to try two free books from another line?
Call 1-800-873-8635 or visit www.ReaderService.com.

* Terms and prices subject to change without notice. Prices do not include applicable taxes. Sales tax applicable in N.Y. Canadian residents will be charged applicable taxes. Offer not valid in Quebec. This offer is limited to one order per household. All orders subject to credit approval. Credit or debit balances in a customer's account(s) may be offset by any other outstanding balance owed by or to the customer. Please allow 4 to 6 weeks for delivery. Offer available while quantities last.

Your Privacy—The Reader Service is committed to protecting your privacy. Our Privacy Policy is available online at www.ReaderService.com or upon request from the Reader Service.

We make a portion of our mailing list available to reputable third parties that offer products we believe may interest you. If you prefer that we not exchange your name with third parties, or if you wish to clarify or modify your communication preferences, please visit us at www.ReaderService.com/consumerchoice or write to us at Reader Service Preference Service, P.O. Box 9062, Buffalo, NY 14269. Include your complete name and address.

HDES11B

red-hot reads

Fall under the spell of fan-favorite author

Leslie Kelly

Workaholic Mimi Burdette thinks she's satisfied dating the
handsome man her father has picked out for her. But when sexy
firefighter Xander McKinley moves into her apartment building,
Mimi finds herself becoming…distracted. When Mimi opens a
fortune cookie predicting who will be the man of her dreams,
then starts having erotic dreams, she never imagines Xander
is having the same dreams! Until they come together
and bring those dreams to life.

Blazing Midsummer Nights

The magic begins June 2012

Saddle up with Harlequin® series books this summer
and find a cowboy for every mood!

Available wherever books are sold.